D0581697

The Big Ranchero

After witnessing the cold-blooded killing of a man named Boyd Larsen, Duke Benedict and Hank Brazos found themselves up to their gunbelts in mystery, murder and mayhem. Someone was rustling cattle from Nate Kendrick's Rancho Antigua, and while that in itself wasn't Benedict and Brazos' business, rumor had it that the man doing all the rustling was Bo Rangle, the cut-throat outlaw they've been tracking ever since he massacred their men in the closing days of the Civil War.

Signing on as range detective and wrangler respectively, Benedict and Brazos set out to run the rustlers to ground and exact their revenge on Rangle. But before they can find the man, they need to find the cattle . . . and somehow or other, those cattle have vanished right off the face of the earth!

The Big Ranchero

E. Jefferson Clay

A Black Horse Western

ROBERT HALE

First published by Cleveland Publishing Co. Pty Ltd,
New South Wales, Australia
First published in 1967

© 2019 by Piccadilly Publishing

This edition © The Crowood Press, 2020

ISBN 978-0-7198-3112-6

The Crowood Press
The Stable Block
Crowood Lane
Ramsbury
Marlborough
Wiltshire SN8 2HR

www.bhwesterns.com

Robert Hale is an imprint
of The Crowood Press

Typeset by Derek Doyle & Associates, Shaw Heath
Printed and bound in Great Britain by
4Bind Ltd, Stevenage, SG1 2XT

ONE

THE NIGHT THE KILLER CAME

The cantina door swung open and Salazar the killer stood there in the yellow lamplight with the night a black frame around him.

The Mexican's coal black eyes swept over the crowded, noisy room, pausing no longer on the man he'd come to kill than on any other. His spurs jingled softly as he crossed to the rough, unplaned bar, breathed 'Tequila,' to Big Fats Arriba.

'Sí, Señor Salazar, sí. It is some time since we see you in Sabinosa, is it not?'

The newcomer made no response. He picked up his drink and took it to a corner table and sat with his back against the wall, scarred face in the shadows.

Big Fats shivered, wishing it was the chill New

Mexico night that made him cold, but knowing it wasn't. He peered through the swirling tobacco smoke at the new arrival to Arriba's Cantina, until Salazar felt his stare and drilled him with a cold, unblinking glare. Big Fats dropped a glass, and bent gruntingly to sweep up the fragments with unsteady hands. When he straightened red-faced, he didn't look over to the corner table again. With flat feet, indigestion, and a bad-tempered wife with a nagging tongue who gave him a calling down every day, the barkeep had all the problems he needed.

Apart from Big Fats who knew all the good, the bad and the ugly in that lawless corner of south-east New Mexico, few denizens of the cantina paid any attention to the latest arrival who'd been blown in by the yammering wind. For Saturday night in Sabinosa was the night you left your worries at home and made your way to Arriba's to forget about the week just done with, and to hell with the new one waiting around Sunday's corner.

Arriba's didn't cater to the fastidious, but it was a big, warm and comfortable enough place to be on a night like this, when the wind-whipped sand blasted angrily at the windows and the whole night was alive and howling. The cantina, which had been a church in the days when Sabinosa believed in God, was some eighty feet long by forty wide, with a low-beamed roof and thick adobe walls. The altar had been converted into a rough stage where a pair of drunken Mexes strummed guitars, and half-naked girls sporadically danced and sang.

The place was dimly lit with six oil lamps hanging low from the rafters over bar, stage and gaming tables, and on crowded nights with the air thick with smoke, it was impossible to see from one end to the other. Still, that only added to the atmosphere the patrons boasted, and nobody was concerned with poor visibility as they drank their rum and tequila, pawed the girls and watched with fascinated interest as the back of Hank Brazos' great fist was forced closer and closer to the burning candle stump waxed to the table.

'You reckon you're hot as a two dollar pistol, don't you, blacksmith?' Brazos grunted as the flame singed the back of his hand. He was a youthful giant of a man with a craggy sun-bronzed face and a great barrel of a chest. 'You reckon you got me beat back-side-to-breakfast?'

'It would seem so, gringo,' Gregorio grinned.

He stopped grinning instantly as the thick slabs of muscle rolled under his opponent's faded purple shirt, and Brazos' hand drove his hairy arm back up towards the vertical.

'Now what do you reckon, blacksmith?'

Seated at the table next to the contestants with the little pile of stake money in front of him, tall, good-looking Duke Benedict saw what was happening and gave a sharp cough. Brazos' hard blue eyes cut to his partner and Benedict imperceptibly shook his head.

Glowering, Brazos turned back to the blacksmith,

then suddenly broke the grip as Gregorio forced his hand down onto the candle.

'You win, blacksmith,' he growled, to a wild chorus of jubilation from the winners packed five deep around the tables.

'First time I've ever seen him bested at wrist-wrestling,' Duke Benedict said with convincing dejection as he paid out the dimes, quarters and centavos to all who'd backed the blacksmith to win. 'Without a doubt, Señor Gregorio, you're an uncommonly powerful man.'

Pas Gregorio, two hundred and sixty pounds of prime Mexican beef with arms like thighs and a face like a badly cooked tortilla, stood up in acknowledgment of the compliment and thumped his mighty chest. There was triumph and relief in the blacksmith's greasy heart, for there for a couple of moments he'd thought he'd felt a truly uncommon strength in the arm of the bigger of the two gringos who had drifted into Sabinosa late that afternoon. But he'd been happily mistaken. Hank Brazos, like every other man he'd ever locked hands with, had folded in the end. A good opponent, but nothing really special.

While Gregorio basked and the debonair Benedict paid out his bets with convincing dejection, Hank Brazos stood moodily to one side twisting a quirley, scowling darkly and avoiding the silent reproof in the eyes of the ugly dog squatting at his feet.

His expression didn't change any when Benedict

came up to him and spoke softly.

'Now this time you win – but not before I say so, understand?'

'Of course I do, dammit. I ain't dumb, am I?'

That was a matter for some debate as far as Benedict was concerned. His partner was in something of a class of his own when it came to some things like reading trails, brawling, raising hell or trading lead, but brainwork was hardly his long suit. Brazos was just as likely to forget that this was just a means of raising folding money, and if that happened they could end up without even the ten dollar 'outlay' Benedict had already paid out.

'Just take it easy,' Benedict advised. 'You and I know he can't beat you, and in a couple of minutes they'll all know. So don't jump the gun.'

'I know what to goddam do,' Brazos growled back, watching Gregorio who was now letting a tarnished cantina angel feel his bicep. 'Let's get on with it.'

Benedict turned to the crowd and announced that, simple-minded fool as he was, he had a final miserable five dollars to wager on a second and final contest – that was, of course, if Señor Gregorio was willing.

Señor Gregorio was more than willing. He quickly resumed his chair and assumed the ready position, elbow on the table, hand outstretched between the two burning candle stubs that were waxed to the table to keep the contestants honest. The Mexicans covered Benedict's five like men who were almost ashamed to take the money, and Brazos sat down opposite Gregorio trying to look like a man beaten before he even began.

Bets covered, Benedict sat down elegantly beside the dancing girl who thought he was bello, and said to the combatants:

'Take the grip!'

They took the grip.

'Commence!'

Gregorio set to with a fine show of strength and immediately brought a roar from the crowd when he forced Brazos' hand down an inch. The hands remained at that level for a sweating, grunting ten seconds, then moved another inch toward Brazos' candle.

'Hah! He is defeated again!' a buck-toothed Mexican laughed at Benedict's elbow.

'Not at all,' Benedict disagreed. 'My partner is simply letting your blacksmith expend his energy.'

Buck-teeth sneered. 'Eef you have such confidence, Señor, then why ees it you do not wager more on your *amigo* than a miserable five dollars?'

Duke Benedict seemed to hesitate at that. He frowned, then with a great show of reluctance, dipped into his vest pocket and produced a beautiful, heavy gold watch. He sighed regretfully, then got up and slid the watch across the bar to Big Fats.

'Barkeep, what will you lend me on my timepiece?'

Big Fats' eyes stretched wide as he picked up the finest looking watch he'd ever seen. But being a thief and usurer to the bone, he immediately looked disinterested as he shrugged.

'Fifty dollars . . . no more.'

'It's worth two hundred and you know it. But very well, Shylock, I'll take it.'

Big Fats couldn't produce the money quickly enough. Benedict left the cash on the bar and said, 'Well, gentlemen, I have a sentimental attachment for my watch, but loyalty demands I support my partner.' He slapped the bar. 'Fifty dollars on the strong right arm of Señor Brazos.'

The result was instant chaos. It seemed everyone in the cantina wanted a share of that fifty dollars. Yelling, pushing and shoving, the mob showered pesos, dimes, quarters, centavos and a few crumpled dollar bills onto the table until the gambling man was forced to call a halt.

'Thank you, gentlemen, thank you,' he beamed, stacking up the loot. 'The good Lord loves the cheerful giver.'

'Por Dios!' whispered little Abrana, the dancer at Benedict's side, her black Spanish eyes fixed with wonder and greed on such a fortune. 'Mi vida, you mus' be crazee. Your companero, he ees fineesh.'

'Correction,' Benedict murmured, lighting up a fresh Havana and leaning back expansively. 'It is Gregorio who is finished.'

Abrana took another look at the combatants. The Americano's hand had dropped another tenth of an inch closer to the flame.

'Fineesh,' she repeated and her bare brown shoulders dropped disconsolately. Until Benedict had cashed his watch, she'd been content enough just simply to share the company of the most handsome gringo ever to step through Arriba's batwings. But such extravagance which could better have been lavished upon her, filled her with depression. How tragic for a man to look so intelligent, yet be so stupid.

Then suddenly the mob's cheers of encouragement for their champion began to fade, and little Abrana gaped. Hank Brazos had just forced Gregorio's hand up a full inch.

Gregorio's swarthy face showed a brief disbelief. Then Sabinosa's best threw everything into the final thrust that would drive Brazos' hand onto the flickering flame.

Brazos' fist didn't budge.

Now there wasn't a sound. Doubt, like an evil shadow, clouded every watching face. Across the trembling fists, Gregorio's uncertain eyes stared at the broad, bronzed face under the shock of wild, yellow hair. Brazos' broad, fist-scarred mouth didn't alter its expression, but in the American's sky-blue eyes, the Mexican strong man saw an unmistakable twinkle.

The gringo was playing with him!

The realization twisted Pas Gregorio's guts. He skinned his lips back from clenched teeth, and mounted a Herculean effort to slam that iron fist back. Always the Americans won ... the Mexican's land, his women, his heritage. This was one time, one gringo who would not win.

Unfortunately, this was no ordinary gringo. Two hundred and twenty pounds of iron, muscle and sinew, big Hank Brazos had cut his eye teeth on men of Gregorio's stamp, had never been bested in a test of strength. And now the big money was on, he slowly and inexorably drove the blacksmith's arm back to the upright position, then beyond it.

A groan was wrenched from Gregorio's strained lips as his hand was driven to within two inches of the flame. Sweat burst from his face as he summoned his final reserves. To no avail. Relentlessly, Brazos powered his locked hand down until the stench of burning flesh began to pollute the smoky air.

'Enough?' Brazos said softly.

'No ... never!'

'Whatever you say, companero,' Brazos murmured, and smashed the beaten man's fist down onto the flame.

'Enough!'

Gregorio's shout of agony ended the contest. Brazos immediately released him and the blacksmith slumped back ashen-faced, clutching his throbbing hand. The victor came erect, shrugged his shoulders loose, then, because Gregorio had fought hard and clean, unknotted the red bandanna from around his throat and wordlessly wrapped it around the blacksmith's hand.

The end had come so unexpectedly and dramatically that nobody seemed to know what to say. With the exception of Duke Benedict.

'A worthy contest of strength,' he pronounced, gathering up his takings. Then getting up and walking to the bar, he pushed a pile of bills at a stunned Big Fats. 'My timepiece, barkeep.'

The saloonkeeper blinked his surprise away and shook his head. Everybody might have lost out, but Big Fats had no intention of doing so.

'Sorry, gringo,' the fat man shrugged, 'but I do not now wish to sell the watch back.'

Benedict's shoulder dipped and suddenly Big Fats found himself looking down the business end of a Colt .45.

'My watch!'

The attention of the onlookers swung from Brazos and Gregorio as Duke Benedict's hard words cut through the room. Most had tabbed Brazos' partner as a dude, but the lightning appearance of the gun forced them to take another look. They read the steel in the gambler's eyes, noted for the first time the breadth of shoulder, the deadly poise and balance of the man that seemed to have escaped them before.

Big Fats' smile was sick. 'Of course, Señor, I make the joke.'

His features a study in cowardly dejection, Arriba produced the watch and handed it over. He'd been wrong about Gregorio being able to beat Hank

14

Brazos, and he'd been wrong in sizing Benedict up as a dude. Maybe it just wasn't his night.

'Well, now that's straightened out,' Hank Brazos grinned as Benedict put gun and timepiece away, 'let's get down to some serious drinkin'.' He draped a heavy arm around the blacksmith's shoulders. 'C'mon, amigo, drinks are on me.'

Up until that moment, the crowd had been silent, stunned by the unexpected outcome of the contest. But the sight of Brazos and Gregorio breasting the bar together jolted them out of their gloom and reminded them that they had seen something special tonight. A battle of strength had been decided with honor, and now also with honor, the former adversaries drank tequila together. Such a noble thing was enough to make a man forget his little problems, and even as a smiling Benedict raked in the winnings, some men shrugged, some smiled philosophically and all moved to the bar to take a little tequila.

All that was, but the haggard-faced American drinking alone along the bar – and the scar-faced man who sat in the shadows watching him.

But nobody paid them the slightest attention, for suddenly, with his arm around Gregorio's shoulders and looking directly at Benedict who was busily stuffing the loot away, Hank Brazos boomed out:

'OK, line up and name your poison, boys. Since we are winners, we're kinda in a generous mood. Ten bucks worth of booze on me and my old pard, Señor Benedict.'

A shout of 'Fire!' could scarcely have caused more upheaval, and it was a full minute before an angry Duke Benedict could extricate himself from the boisterous, back-slapping mob of grateful drinkers, and haul Brazos clear to give him a piece of his mind.

'Are you clean out of that lump of granite you call a head?' he hissed, gesticulating at the cantina's clients who were tramping one another into the boards to get at the free stuff. 'Why in the holy name of sweet Judas H. Iscariot did you . . . ?'

'Simmer down, Yank, simmer down,' Brazos grinned. 'We can afford a few bucks' worth of booze.'

'Afford? Goddammit what do you think . . .?'

'Look, hold your tongue a minute will you. We took these wetbacks, Yank, and they ain't even smart enough to know they been took. A buck's mighty hard to come by down in this neck of the woods, and some of these tortilla eaters lost more than they could afford. We got our stake, Yank, so leave us not be greedy, huh?'

Scathing words came to Duke Benedict's lips, but died there. He looked at the drinkers – they reminded him of orphans at a rich man's Christmas; it might have been ten years or never since they'd been treated to free liquor.

'You know maybe you're right,' he said after a long moment.

'Of course I'm right.' Brazos grinned around his cigarette and clapped him on the shoulder. 'C'mon, Yank, it's been a long, hard day. Leave us get ourselves around some of this booze.'

They headed for the bar together, and only then sighted the scar-faced Mexican drinking alone in the corner.

'Hey!' Brazos called, 'didn't you hear, Mex? Free rotgut. Tequila. Savvy?'

The man just stared, but made no move, no response.

'Hey, I said we're buyin'.' Brazos was not grinning now. 'That means everybody.'

The scar-faced man drew deep on a cigarillo, exhaled a contemptuous cloud of smoke towards them. Brazos growled and made towards the table, but Benedict held his arm.

'Leave him be, Reb.'

'But dammitall, that's an insult.'

'So it's an insult,' Benedict said softly. 'So if you hang around a dump like this long enough, you'd get insulted every morning before breakfast. Besides, he looks like bad news to me.'

'I'll . . .'

Brazos broke off as Cindy, one of the dancers, came undulating out of the crowd to take them by the arm. 'Come on, caballeros,' she purred, giving Brazos a little tickle in the ribs, 'it is bad manners for the hosts not to drink with the guests, is it not?'

Brazos didn't know enough about manners to fit in a bug's ear, but he did know that little Cindy was a country mile better looking than old hatchet-face in the corner. He shot the silent figure one final look over his shoulder, then grinned at the girl and gestured towards the bar.

'Why, lead the way then, little lady, lead the way. I'd rather be a dead coon in a post hole than bad mannered, wouldn't you, Reb?'

'Oh, any time, any time,' Duke Benedict agreed, and arm in arm they sashayed up to the bar where Big Fats had their drinks already waiting, a whisky for Benedict, beer for Brazos, gin for pretty Cindy.

And nothing for the man in the corner.

TWO

COLD STEEL

By the time the ten dollars had cut out and every-body was drinking on his own money, it was plain as paint that it was going to be a big night. It wasn't the sort of thing that could be planned, but once it got under way there was no holding it. In Sabinosa there were nights when you had to laugh, nights when you had to cry. And there were nights too, whether you be impoverished towner, weary vaquero, drifter, bum, whore, dice-player or money-saver, lover, misfit, hero or innocent, you just busted loose.

This was such a night.

Within an hour, the cantina's big night was picking up real momentum. The room rocked with argu-ment, rough laughter, voices lifted in song, the twang of Spanish guitars, the drum of dancing feet. Duke

19

Benedict, with pockets nicely bulging, got up to perform as stylish a fandango with little Abrana as one could wish to see. Brazos played a sad cowboy song on his harmonica that brought big round tears to sentimental Big Fats' eyes, while Pas Gregorio, feeling no pain after half a bottle of free tequila, got up on the bar and did an erratic, but courageous jig.

It was only when one of Gregorio's boots spilled his whisky that Boyd Larsen decided it was time to leave. The man was weary and spent from travel. He had meant to spend the night at Sabinosa before heading on to Summit. But whisky had revived him somewhat, and he was in no mood for hilarity. If he headed out now, he decided, putting on his hat, he could be in Summit by noon.

Somebody jostled the man as he headed for the doors. He looked into the black, hostile eyes of the scar-faced man whom he'd seen come in an hour back.

'Sorry, friend,' he murmured and made to move on.

'Gringo pig!'

Larsen stopped again. He was a tall, raw-boned man of forty with a lean, hard face. His work often took him into danger and he wasn't a man to back away from trouble.

'I said I was sorry, friend.'

Salazar's scarred face twisted in a snarl.

'You gringo cochinos may trample us in your towns, but here you should tread more carefully.

20

Here it is not wise to be so careless.'

A silence began to spread out from the two men now, engulfing the sounds of revelry. There had been arguments aplenty in the past boisterous hour, but they had been drunken, light-hearted incidents, all stemming from high spirits. This sounded like something different.

'What's eatin' you, Mex?' Larsen growled in the growing quiet. 'You lookin' for trouble?'

The Mexican was hunting trouble, but it was the kind of trouble ridiculously out of proportion to a bump in a crowd.

'I grow weary of being bullied by gringo scum!' Salazar hissed, fingering the butt of the wicked-looking knife in his belt. 'Perhaps a man should take a stand somewhere.' He nodded his head as if coming to a decision. 'Si, a man should take a stand . . . now. Tell me, gringo scum, can you use that gun you carry, or is it just there to make cowards of us who cannot afford such fine weapons?'

By this, there was scarcely a sound to be heard in the whole puzzled saloon, and none was more puzzled than Boyd Larsen himself. For Larsen suddenly realized that this was not just a drunken Mex looking for diversion, but a man out for blood.

But why? The question posed itself in his brain, but before he could air it, the scar-faced Mexican spat full in his face.

Larsen's fist dropped to his gun butt as he whipped his coat-sleeve across his face. 'You filthy greaser,' he snarled. 'By God if you were totin' iron I'd kill you for that!'

Salazar smiled a lethal smile and backed away. Men jumped aside to give him room. Ten feet from Larsen he halted, again fingering the hilt of his dagger.

'A gun is your weapon, gringo, the blade is mine.' His voice was soft but there was an edge to it sharper than any knife. 'Let us commence.'

'You're . . . you're goin' to fight me with a knife?' Larsen said incredulously. 'A knife against a gun?'

'Please,' pleaded Big Fats, a man who had seen Salazar and that blade at work once before. 'Please, *companeros*, let us have no more. . . .'

'Shut your fat mouth!' Salazar snarled, and now his voice was no longer soft as he spread his feet and touched the handle of the knife as if it were a live thing. 'Defend yourself, scum!'

Boyd Larsen's hand blurred fast. It closed over the walnut butt of his Colt, wrenched it from leather. He swung the gun up, conscious of the Mexican's whipping right hand, his chilling smile. Something flashed in the yellow light like a darting insect, and a white-hot lance of pain pierced his chest, transfixing him. He was only dimly aware of the thud of his gun hitting the floor, had no way of knowing he was staggering like a drunk with both hands clasped helplessly about the scrolled haft of the dagger embedded to the hilt in his chest. All he was really conscious of, was the grinning scar-face swimming in

22

a haze of fierce yellow light, the incredible pain that filled the world.

Then nothing.

Nobody moved, nobody seemed to breathe as the thud of the falling body faded away. They were all accustomed to violence here, and Duke Benedict and Hank Brazos even more so. But this was something else, and the two manhunters were as stunned as anybody by what had happened.

Until Salazar jingled forward to jerk his knife free and wipe it on the dead man's jacket.

Only then did Brazos give vent to a dangerous growl, toss his drink aside and start towards Salazar. Benedict, standing some short distance away, read his companion's expression and leapt forward, snaring him with a restraining hand.

'Back off, Reb,' he rapped. 'This is no concern of ours.'

'But dammit, you saw how he killed that man, Yank. With a stinkin' knife.'

'It was a fair fight.'

Brazos growled again, but held back, knowing Benedict was right. The two men had fought by the rules of a code he himself lived by, and the man with the gun had had his fair chance. But by glory, it left a dirty taste in a man's mouth to see a fellow-American cut down by a dirty Mex knifer, even if it had been a fair fight.

Salazar's eyes moved to the tall Americans as he came erect, sheathing the blade. There was mockery and challenge in the sharp smile he flicked at them. Then without a word, he turned and jingled to the doors, shouldered through and was instantly gone, the sound of his spurs swallowed by the howl of the wind.

Everybody stood silent as Benedict and Brazos went to the dead man. He'd been American their faces said; it was better Americans should see to him.

'Is there an undertaker in this town?' Benedict said finally after closing the staring eyes.

There was, they assured him, Manuel Chaves, three doors up the main stem. Benedict nodded to Brazos, they hefted the dead man and carried him out.

They were half-blinded by dust and sand by the time they reached the funeral parlor to find the undertaker absent. They carried the corpse into a small, shuttered room and stretched him on a marble-topped bench.

'Shore don't seem right to see a man done in that-away,' Brazos muttered, folding his arms across his steel-ribbed barrel of a chest and looking down at the dead face. 'Wonder who the hell he is?'

Silently, Benedict put his hand in a blood-soaked pocket and extracted a leather wallet. Wiping the wallet dry with a kerchief, he opened it and tugged out a card. It read:

BOYD LARSEN – SOUTHWEST INSURANCE – SUMMIT

Benedict grunted and leafed through a small

diary. 'Seems as if he was investigating a claim on rustled stock on . . .' He paused to decipher bad handwriting. 'On Rancho Antigua it looks like.'

'Yeah, that's one helluva big place down south of here nigh the border. Anythin' else?'

Benedict scanned several more pages crammed with notes and dates. It wasn't until he came to the very last page that he stiffened.

'What is it, Yank?' demanded Brazos. He peered intently over his shoulder at the notebook, despite the fact that he could neither read nor write. 'What's it say?'

Benedict shook his head wonderingly as he read: 'May 23rd. Interviewed Keechez at Candelaria. Fifty pesos for information. Named Rangle. Difficult to believe, but man seems genuine. Warrants personal visit back to Summit.'

'Rangle!' Hank Brazos breathed. 'You sure that's what it says, Yank?'

Benedict took another look. 'Dead sure.'

'Well, I'll be a dirty name.'

'Why, so will I, Reb, so will I.'

It was an hour later when Benedict and Brazos came out of Arriba's again and beat their way across the street through choking clouds of wind-tossed sand to the creaky timber edifice that only in Sabinosa could have been called a hotel. They went directly to Benedict's room, turned up the grease lamp and lit up.

'Well?' grunted Brazos. 'What'd you come up with?'

'Not a great deal. Big Fats says that this Salazar is a notorious thief and killer from the south. He has only seen him once or twice before.'

'He know where he hails from?'

'Just Spanish Valley he said.'

'That's a big place. Arriba have any idea why he killed Larsen?'

'No. But he did say Salazar doesn't particularly need a reason. Our worthy saloonkeeper enlightened me with the rather memorable information, that Salazar once cut a man's throat for breaking wind.'

'Nice feller.'

'A prince. How did you get on at the livery?'

Brazos leaned back in his rickety chair.

'Miguelito the liveryman said Larsen hit town about half an hour after us. Larsen's hoss was played out and he told Miguelito he aimed to stay in town the night to spell his cayuse. The Mex said Larsen looked like he needed a good spell himself.'

Benedict drew thoughtfully on his fine Havana. 'I believe Salazar came here specifically to kill Larsen,' he said at length. 'He most likely trailed him up from the south.'

'Does it matter a damn one way or the other?' Brazos challenged, pacing slowly up and down with the table lamps flinging his shadow huge on walls and ceiling. 'It's Bo Rangle we're interested in, not any greaser knifer.'

Indeed it was, Duke Benedict acknowledged with a nod of his dark head. It was a long and dangerous trail that had brought them to Sabinosa on the faint scent of former guerilla leader Bo Rangle. Six months back at a bloody place called Pea Ridge, Georgia, in the dying days of the War of the States, Federal Captain Duke Benedict's unit had attacked Confederate Sergeant Hank Brazos' platoon attempting to get clear of the battle zone with two hundred thousand dollars' worth of Confederate gold to Mexico. Both squads were all but decimated, when Rangle's Raiders struck and bore the fortune away. By chance, in the days of turmoil following Appomattox, the two men who'd fought so savagely against each other, then even more fiercely together against Bo Rangle, had met and joined forces to search for the gold, which was believed to be still intact in some secret cache, where Rangle had as yet been unable to return.

The trail had proven long and hard, for Bo Rangle, killer, traitor and thief, was a man of infinite guile and cunning, and this was their first whiff of a decent lead on their quarry in too many searching weeks.

As such, they meant to make the most of it, though until Duke Benedict laid out the plan of action, Brazos didn't know exactly how. The one thing the big man was ready to concede about the 'Yank,' apart from his unquestioned reserve of guts, was that he had a tolerably good head on his shoulders – for a tinhorn gambling man with a foreign accent, that was.

'We'll ride up to Summit tomorrow and see Larsen's superior at Southwest Insurance,' Benedict decided after a thoughtful half-cigar of silence. 'He should be able to fill in the gaps of what we don't know.'

Brazos shrugged. That was OK by him. He was happy enough just so long as things were moving. It was sitting about that got him in a twist.

'After we've seen the insurance company,' Benedict went on, stubbing out his stogie, 'why, I do believe we shall find ourselves heading south to take a first-hand look at Rancho Antigua? That sound all right to you, Reb?'

It did, and later when he'd returned to his own room, fed Bullpup, his dog, and shucked off boots and gunbelt and stood by his closed window looking out at the blowing night, Hank Brazos was aware of an old familiar tingling in his blood. The last time he'd felt that sensation had been in a little Colorado cowtown named Daybreak, just before they'd flushed Bo Rangle from hiding and buried half the town when he finally got away again.

Brazos drew deeply on his weed and his thoughts drifted back to that crimson day of battle when so many sons of the brave South had died because of Bo Rangle – and of all those who'd died since – as Boyd Larsen most likely had.

He hoped that tingle in his bones wasn't fooling. If it wasn't, then maybe this would be the trail that would finally lead them, not only to the Confederate gold, but to vengeance.

Henry Gordon had a nice little wife who mothered him, a sensitive stomach, a great deal of money and an insurance company. He also had a surprise awaiting him when he reached his office in Summit that morning after wiring funds to Sabinosa to cover the burial of his murdered agent, Boyd Larsen.

Gordon's manner was heavy and preoccupied as he pushed through the frosted glass doors of his office and made his way down the aisle between the rows of desks where his female clerks were already at work. Had he been less preoccupied, Gordon would have noticed that there was more than a suggestion of distraction amongst his staff. As it was, he didn't become aware of anything untoward until he was opening the little gate that led into the railed-off area occupied by his two private secretaries and almost tripped over a monster sprawled out leisurely on the rug.

Henry Gordon's uncertain stomach flipped and he'd gone a good three feet backwards in one startled jump before he realized that it was only a dog.

Or at least it looked like a dog, though unlike any dog he'd ever seen in his life. It was a massive-shouldered creature of a dirty white color, marked by big brown splotches. Its great head was a combination of bulldog and mastiff, its mouth looked about a foot across and two yellow eyes set towards the top of its head stared up at the trembling Gordon with a bleak and challenging hostility.

Somehow the managing director of Southwest Insurance managed to drag his eyes away from the incredible beast as his two private secretaries, plump and pretty Miss Hunter, and skinny and spinsterish Miss Mathews came hurrying forward.

'Oh, Mr. Gordon,' the elderly Miss Mathews greeted him, plainly distressed. 'Thank heavens you've arrived. We've been having an absolutely terrible morning!'

'Oh, it hasn't really been that bad,' Miss Hunter disagreed. She stepped around the dog and opened the gate for him. 'Come on in, Mr. Gordon, he won't hurt you.'

The girl reached for his arm to guide him around the dog, but he pulled away and made his way gingerly around the beast unaided. Only now, as he recovered from the shock of finding a man-eater sprawled across his secretaries' floor at nine-fifteen on a Monday morning, was Henry Gordon growing aware of the fact that everybody seemed to be staring at him expectantly instead of getting on with their work.

Adjusting his spectacles and putting a calming hand on his alarmed stomach, he fixed his secretaries with a severe stare.

'Miss Mathews, Miss Hunter – just what is going

on here?'

Before either woman could reply, Gordon received his second rude shock in as many minutes when the door of his private office swung open and two total strangers stepped out.

Gordon bristled. This was too much!

'Miss Mathews,' he snapped angrily. 'Who are these persons?'

'Benedict is the name,' said the tall, black-haired man in the suit, stepping forward. 'Mr. Gordon?'

'Yes, this is Mr. Gordon, Mr. Benedict,' young Miss Hunter supplied, and Gordon couldn't help but notice how she dimpled at the man. 'Mr. Gordon, Mr. Benedict and his friend have been waiting to see you since 8.15. We, well I really mean Miss Mathews, decided to have them wait in your office as they seemed to be distracting the staff.'

Gordon could believe that. The man named Benedict was handsome enough to distract a convent full of holy nuns, while his towering, ox-shouldered companion in the purple shirt was eye-catching to say the least.

'A great pleasure, Mr. Gordon,' Benedict said with a flashing smile and gave a little bow. He gestured negligently. 'My . . . er, associate, Mr. Hank Brazos.'

'Howdy,' drawled the giant.

Henry Gordon took a neatly folded silk kerchief from his breast pocket and gently patted his forehead – then jumped a foot as the dog which he'd just about forgotten barked at nothing in particular and shook the room.

'Shut up, ugly,' Brazos said. Then with a grin to Gordon. 'He don't like bein' indoors. Makes him ornery.'

'Perhaps there is some feasible explanation of this . . . this flagrant breach of office decorum,' Gordon said with as much dignity as he could muster, 'but if there is, I don't wish to hear it. Miss Mathews and Miss Hunter, I shall deal with you later. Now, if you will both be so good as to take your leave.'

'Mr. Gordon shore knows some big words, Yank,' Brazos observed. His brow creased. 'What's he sayin'?'

'I am saying,' Gordon snapped out, 'that you men are to leave my office immediately.'

'But, sir. . . .' Benedict started to protest, but Gordon cut him off.

'Immediately I say sir, I have neither time nor patience to argue.'

'But, Mr. Gordon,' Miss Hunter got in, 'Mr. Benedict and Mr. Brazos have come to see you about Mr. Larsen.'

Gordon stared.

'Is this true?'

'Shore is,' Brazos confirmed. 'We seen your man get kilt in Sabinosa, mister.'

'It was us who carried Larsen's body to the funeral parlor, Mr. Gordon,' Benedict told him. 'Now, do we talk?'

'We most certainly do,' Henry Gordon replied,

32

and the sober change in the man was remarkable as he stepped firmly to his door and swung it open. 'After you, gentlemen. And Miss Mathews, I am not to be disturbed.'

It took Duke Benedict less than ten minutes to tell the story. He left nothing out, added nothing. Seated behind his big, highly polished desk, Gordon listened attentively to every word.

When Benedict was through, he shook his head sadly from side to side.

'So it was a deliberate killing you believe, Mr. Benedict? Not just a brawl?'

'Not from where I was standing,' Benedict said, and looked at Brazos.

'The Mex was out to nail Larsen,' Brazos confirmed. 'Your man didn't stand a prayer.'

Gordon nodded sadly. 'I knew it had to be something like that. Boyd Larsen was one of the Southwest's best men. He would never get involved in a barroom brawl.'

'I took the liberty of reading this in Sabinosa, Mr. Gordon,' Benedict said, producing Larsen's diary. He opened the book and passed it across. 'Would you read that last entry please?'

Gordon scanned the handwritten lines and gasped.

'Bo Rangle!'

'Bo Rangle,' Benedict confirmed, leaning forward. 'And that's what brings us here, Mr. Gordon. We're interested in that desperado.'

'Mighty interested,' Brazos grunted.

Gordon met Benedict's eyes that had suddenly grown cold. He glanced across at Hank Brazos and the big man's face had set in hard lines and planes. Gordon nodded to himself. He understood. A renegade murderer such as Bo Rangle would have made a thousand bitter foes. These two formidable-looking men could well be amongst the marauder's most dangerous enemies.

Things were beginning to add up for Gordon now. He'd sensed that men like these wouldn't have made the long ride from Sabinosa just to express their sympathy for Larsen.

He said, 'I take it then, gentlemen, that you have come to see me in the hope of gleaning further information on Rangle?'

'Possibly, Mr. Gordon,' Benedict said. 'Now, what can you tell us?'

'Nothing.'

Their faces fell.

'Nothin'?' Brazos echoed.

Gordon shook his head. 'I'm sorry, gentlemen, I don't know a thing about Bo Rangle or his movements.' He tapped the diary with his finger. 'This, in fact, is the first time I've heard the man's name mentioned in months, I suppose.'

Benedict and Brazos exchanged a glum glance. Brazos said, 'Well, what about tellin' us what Larsen was up to down at Rancho Antigua, Gordon? Mebbe from that we can add somethin' up?'

'Well, there's nothing secret and nothing particularly unusual about the investigation,' Gordon supplied. 'Rancho Antigua is a client of ours. They've been losing cattle. Mr. Nathan Kendrick filed an insurance claim and it was only a formality for us to send Larsen down there to investigate and verify the cattle's disappearance before payment was made.'

'Is that all there is to it?' said Benedict.

'Well, not exactly. Larsen reported back that though there seemed little doubt that the cattle were in fact missing, nobody seemed to be able to find out how or where they'd gone. Larsen was working on this aspect of the matter when I received his last and final report.'

A heavy silence enveloped the room. Over the transom, drifted the busy sounds of industry; the employees of Southwest Insurance were belatedly getting on with the morning's work.

Finally Brazos moved to a window and looked out over the weathered walls and rooftops of Summit. 'Well, what do you aim to do about Larsen, Gordon?'

Henry Gordon slumped a little in his chair. 'I haven't decided, to be perfectly honest. Larsen was one of our best and toughest field men. We're very short of men of that stamp right at the moment, and the few we do have are all out investigating various claims. I'm very much afraid I shall have to wait until Johnston or Kilraine become available to send them down to Rancho Antigua to resume the investigation. It galls me to have to delay such a matter, for it's quite obvious to me that Larsen had discovered something and was most probably killed because of it.'

'That is how it seems to add up,' Benedict said. He paused to take out a silver cigar case and select a Havana. He was very thoughtful as he said, 'Tell me, Mr. Gordon, what are the qualifications needed to become a field man for Southwest Insurance?'

'Well, a man must be physically fit, intelligent, reliable, dedicated . . .' Gordon looked at Benedict closely. 'But why do you ask, Mr. Benedict?'

Benedict smiled around his cigar. 'Why, that description Mr. Gordon just gave sounds almost like a rundown on us, wouldn't you say, Reb?'

Brazos blinked, not understanding.

Neither did Henry Gordon until Benedict explained, 'Mr. Gordon, we want to come to grips with Bo Rangle, and you want Boyd Larsen's death investigated. Why don't we combine forces?'

'Combine forces? I don't understand.'

'Send us South as your new representative, sir.'

Negatives rose up in Henry Gordon but died before reaching his lips. Thoughtfully he looked from one man to the other. Despite looks, charm and education, Duke Benedict was quite obviously not a Southwest man – and his friend was quite impossible. But could he afford to be so particular? Whatever their shortcomings, he couldn't deny they were a formidable looking pair . . . perhaps they were exactly the type of investigators, who should be sent to continue the investigation of Rancho Antigua, more particularly if infamous Bo Rangle were somehow involved.

There were those who said that Henry Gordon was a stuffed-shirt, a slave to red tape, fussy, pedantic and pernickety in business matters, yet despite these things which were, in the main, true, he was also capable of swift decision when the occasion demanded. He made such a decision then, after just half a minute of deliberation.

'All right . . . all right, Mr. Benedict sir, by heaven I do think you might be just the man I need. But I must warn you of the dangers involved. You won't be handsomely paid and after what happened to Larsen, there is no guarantee that . . .'

'You can skip all that, Mr. Gordon,' Benedict cut him off. 'If it comes right down to cases I guess I'd rather live with danger than without it. Now let's get down to business, shall we?'

They did just that, and by the time Miss Mathews came in thirty minutes later, Duke Benedict was a properly authorized and informed Insurance Inspector, equipped with the necessary papers and identification to enable him to act on behalf of Southwest Insurance in a matter of the investigation, firstly of the Rancho Antigua's rustled beeves and secondly of the killing of field man Boyd Larsen.

'Yes, Miss Mathews, what is it?' Gordon said, as Benedict and Brazos made ready to leave.

'I'm sorry to interrupt, Mr. Gordon,' the woman said, 'but Miss Larsen is here.'

Gordon's face fell. Brazos asked, 'Miss Larsen? She kin to Boyd Larsen?'

'His sister,' Gordon informed. 'A lovely young woman, quite attached to her brother. Doubtless she has come for details of his death.' He spread his hands. 'It will really be very difficult for me to talk to her. These sorts of things sound very impersonal when all you can give are the bare, hard facts.'

'Mebbe we could talk to her,' said Brazos.

They looked at him.

'Well,' he shrugged, 'we seen it happen. Mebbe it would be easier on the little lady if we could tell her how it happened, how he died quick and got took care of proper, afterwards.'

'Why, that's a very kind offer, Mr. Brazos,' Gordon said, 'and I do believe it would help to . . .'

'Now just a minute,' Benedict broke in. 'Mr. Gordon is in a better position to do it, besides we've got to be moving.'

'Won't take long,' Brazos argued. 'And I reckon it'd mean a lot to the little gal to talk to someone who was there, Yank.'

'Well, I suppose it would be a Christian kindness,' Benedict decided. 'You talk to the girl and I'll go see to the horses and meet you out front in ten minutes.'

'Right,' Brazos grunted. He slouched out, kicked Bullpup awake, then followed Miss Mathews through to the waiting room to meet Miss Helen Larsen.

THREE

BRAZOS COMES CALLING

Brazos leant down and fed Bullpup a cream cake. It vanished without a trace and the hound licked his chops with a startlingly pink tongue, that had the texture of sandpaper. When Brazos looked up again, the girl was smiling for the first time.

'You like dogs, Miss Larsen?'

'Yes I do . . . particularly yours Mr. Brazos. He has . . . well, character.'

'Nobody's ever said that about him afore, but I guess you're right at that. Another cup of coffee?'

'No, thank you. But I really do feel much better now.'

The big man nodded, and poured himself another cup of black. They were seated by the window of the

Silver Spoon Eatery almost opposite the offices of Southwest Insurance. It had been Brazos' idea to leave the office which had to have painful associations for the girl, and the idea seemed to have been successful. The girl had been tearful at the office when he'd told her about Sabinosa, but coffee and a change of scene seemed to have lifted her spirits. She was a brave girl in Brazos' book, pretty too, with shoulder-length blonde hair and the blue eyes and fine complexion of her Scandinavian stock.

'Mr. Brazos?'

'Yes, missy?'

'This man who killed my brother – Salazar you said his name was? What will happen to him now? Will he just . . . well, get away with it?'

'I doubt it, missy. You see, me and my partner are takin' up down south, where your brother left off. Gordon's hired us to follow up your brother's work on Rancho Antigua and see if we can't run that Mex to ground too. As a matter of fact, me and my partner are headin' south when we leave here. Seems that's where this Salazar jasper hails from.'

The girl showed her surprise. 'You an insurance investigator? I don't mean to be rude, Mr. Brazos, but you don't—'

'Don't seem to quite fit?' he grinned. 'No, I reckon that's true enough, but Benedict talked Gordon into puttin' us on, and mebbe between us we can handle her.'

Helen Larsen studied the big man as he spoke.

40

Her first impression of Hank Brazos had been that of a big, shambling, almost sleepy-looking man in dusty range garb, most likely an out-of-work cowboy or simple drifter. But the more she studied him the more she sensed that there was a deal more to him than that. There was a tremendous suggestion of latent power under his easy-going way, a lazy alertness in his brilliant blue eyes. She saw the way the heavy slabs of chest and shoulder muscle rippled under the purple shirt as he built himself a cigarette and noticed, too, the small white scar on his bronzed face that spoke of violence and danger.

The overall impression was that of a man who could do almost anything he set out to do, and that realization prompted her to say,

'Mr. Brazos, do you think you could do something for me?'

'Anything you say, missy.'

She leant forward, blue eyes intense. 'Please try and bring Boyd's killer to justice. Perhaps it won't help – but will you try, if it's at all possible?'

Hank Brazos' sense of chivalry was touched. 'Miss Larsen, you've got my word.'

She touched his hand in gratitude, then looked up sharply as a tall, dark-haired man strode into the eatery and crossed to their table.

Brazos grinned and got to his feet. 'Oh, sorry, Yank, clean forgot all about you. Er, this here is Miss Helen Larsen.'

The girl acknowledged the introduction, but

seemed totally immune to Benedict's polished charm, and actually took Brazos' arm as they quit the eatery and headed across to the hitch rack where the horses were waiting. Helen Larsen was a lovely young woman, Benedict decided, but obviously had no taste at all.

'*Adios*, Miss Helen,' Brazos said with a salute as they mounted up. 'You'll be hearin' from me.'

'What was all that about?' Benedict demanded as they rode out.

Brazos turned in the saddle and waved to the slim, erect figure on the insurance office porch as they swung out of the main street.

'Well?' Benedict pressed.

Brazos didn't answer as they crossed the Concho River Bridge and struck south across the Apache Plains. This was just something between he and Boyd Larsen's sister. Whichever way things went down in Spanish Valley, he was going to see Salazar the killer either dead or in chains. He'd given his word.

Lash Fallon said, 'Shut up that whistlin', Mex. You reckon I want to listen to that all day?'

Leaning lazily against the two-rail fence on a hilltop beside the main trail into Rancho Antigua where the two hands were standing morning lookout, little Manuelita Orlando shrugged with the eloquence of his race.

'It helps to pass the time.'

'Fifty goddam hands on the goddam place, and I

got to draw you,' mouthed Fallon. A tall, high-shoul-
dered man with a hawk nose and bright red hair,
Lash Fallon was foul-tempered by nature and his
mood this morning even more acid than usual. On
Rancho Antigua, standing lookout was rated just a
cut above mucking out stables, and it wasn't
improved by sharing the chore with a greaser. Fallon
didn't like Mexicans. He particularly didn't like
whistling Mexicans.

'Tobacco?' Orlando suggested, proffering his
pouch in an attempt to coax Fallon out of his sour
mood.

'Go to hell,' Fallon snapped back and moved some
distance away along the fence, pointedly taking out
his own packet of Bull Durham.

Orlando shrugged indifferently, built a corn shuck
cigarette, lit it and let his eyes play over the familiar
green vastness of Rancho Antigua.

It was springtime in Spanish Valley and the whole
land seemed to blossom in the morning sunlight.
There was April grass underfoot, with April sunlight
dappling through aspens and cottonwoods onto the
sleek red backs of cattle strung out along the gentle
slopes of the hills, and crickets and cicadas vied for
supremacy with the lowing of cows with new calves.

Just visible to the south, the Rancho Antigua's
headquarters stood on a broad flat hilltop, with the
undulating rangeland spread all around. The main
homestead, a massive structure, which had been built
by the former Mexican owner of the Antigua, faced

the east with a five-acre orchard directly behind it. Apart from the house itself which boasted twenty rooms, there was a raft of other buildings, bunkhouses, barns, stables, harness shacks, corn sheds, cook house, corrals. If a stranger were to ride up without knowledge of where he was, one glance at the Antigua headquarters would be all he'd need to know he had to be on one of the most prosperous spreads in southeastern New Mexico.

Manuelita Orlando never got tired of the scenery from up here. Orlando's father had worked the Antigua before him, and his father before him. The little Mex was illiterate, owned no land of his own and never would own any, yet this was his home as much as it was the Kendricks'. Orlando knew every acre of the Antigua, from the towering ramparts of the Bucksaws to the south, to the main ranch gate some six miles north of the hill, and only a couple of miles south of Arroyo. He knew it and loved it and couldn't understand why Fallon seemed disgusted and offended by everything that met his eyes this fine sunny morning.

He didn't attempt to find out however, for Fallon's violent nature was well known on Antigua, particularly to the Mexican hands on the ranch.

It was almost time for the noon meal, the little vaquero decided, looking up at the sun as he turned his back on the headquarters and looked the other way along the main trail leading out. Maybe after meat and coffee, Fallon would be in a better mood and feel like talking. Talking helped to pass the time on sentry guard.

The Mexican realized he'd been watching the progress of the solitary rider coming along the trail for some time before it suddenly dawned on him that he wasn't a Rancho Antigua man.

There was no hurry or alarm about Orlando as he strolled up the fence to tell Fallon. A man coming in broad daylight was hardly suspicious.

Lash Fallon had other ideas about that. 'The boss never said he was expectin' nobody today,' he growled, narrowed eyes focused on the approaching horseman. 'C'mon, we'll turn him 'round.'

Orlando felt a twinge of apprehension as he forked his cayuse with the careless grace of the born horseman and followed Fallon's broad back down the slope. He'd seldom seen Fallon in such a violent mood. He could smell trouble.

Hank Brazos caught a whiff of it too, as the two riders came swiftly down through the lush hillside grass towards the trail. After he and Benedict had decided he should try and get himself a job on the big ranchero in nearby Arroyo that morning, they'd asked around some and had learned that the Antigua was leery of strangers, following the recent heavy rustling raids. He didn't want to get on the wrong side before he got started, so he reined in under a trailside cottonwood, kept his hands well away from his gun and put on an amiable grin as the cowboy and the vaquero cut the trail fifty yards ahead, then rode towards him.

The cowboy astride the long-legged bay had a hot, angry look to him, his right hand riding his gun butt. The Mexican looked tame enough he noted as they dragged their horses to a dusty halt before him.

'Howdy, gents. You Rancho Antigua boys?'

'What's it to you, saddle bum?' snarled Fallon.

'Why, I figured if you was, you might direct me to the ranch house. Brazos is the name. Hank Brazos.'

'Si, we are of the Antigua,' the little Mexican supplied. 'I am Manuelita Orlando, and my companero is Lash Fallon. You have business with the rancho, Señor Brazos?'

'Shut up! I'll do the goddam talkin', Mex,' Fallon snapped. The hot, red-rimmed eyes stared at Brazos. 'All right saddle bum, turn that spotted jackass about and git the way you come.'

'Now take it easy, friend,' Brazos said. 'I ain't lookin' for trouble . . . jest want to see your boss man is all.'

Fallon moved his horse closer, a dangerous glint in his eyes.

'You ain't seein' nobody. Our job's to keep strangers offen the Antigua, and that's exactly what we aim to do. Now dust!'

Brazos' grin was getting hard to hold. Mr. Lash Fallon was beginning to rub his neck hair up the wrong way.

He managed to keep an edge out of his voice when he replied. 'Friend, like I say, I'm not lookin'

46

for trouble. All I'm lookin' for is a job.'

'There ain't no jobs here for saddle bums.'

The grin finally gave up and faded away.

'Well, that's too bad. But seein' I come this far, I might as well talk to Mr. Kendrick anyway.'

'You're seein' nobody!' Fallon hissed, and it was plain to see his temper was out of control. 'For the last time, damn you, get off the Antigua or I'll kick you off.'

Hank Brazos went very still in the saddle. The blue eyes turned a deeper color, and to those who knew him well, that meant he was getting riled.

'You'll kick me off, cowboy?'

'You're damned right.'

'I'm gonna see you do it.'

A curse exploded through Fallon's yellow teeth, the gun flashed.

Brazos was expecting it. With lightning speed his left hand lashed out and wrapped in an iron grip about Fallon's wrist. Fallon snarled a curse that turned into a scream of agony as Brazos' right hand swept over filled with gun and the barrel smashed across his arm, snapping it like a stick. Ashen with agony, Fallon grabbed at a knife in his belt.

Brazos swung again. The gun barrel caught the jutting slab of forehead over Fallon's right eye, split it wide and spilled the man unconscious from the saddle.

Manuelita Orlando's eyes threatened to bug from their sockets as the big blue barrel swung to him. His

hands shot up so hard they dislodged his great sombrero which fell to the ground and rolled in a
cartwheel around Fallon's unconscious form.

Brazos held the gun on the Mex for a long
moment, then spun it on his forefinger and plopped
it back into the leather.

'I never come lookin' for trouble, Manuelita. Your
pard gave me no choice.'

'*Si si*, I understand.'

'You sure you do?'

'*Sí, sí.*'

'All right, drop your paws and give me a hand to
get him across his saddle.'

Orlando was so shaken that he was of absolutely
no use at all in getting Fallon up. Brazos handled the
chore himself and when the unconscious wrangler
was draped across his saddle, passed the lines to the
Mexican and motioned him to mount up.

'All right, *companero*,' Brazos said, mounting up
and snapping his fingers to Bullpup who'd obedi-
ently taken no part in the violence. 'Now what say we
ride in easy like and see Mr. Kendrick?'

Orlando moved, riding rigid in the saddle, not
game to look back over his shoulder, not even daring
to brush away the flies for fear the giant gringo might
misunderstand.

But the Mexican had nothing to fear. Hank Brazos
was a peaceable man by nature – until somebody got
to rubbing him up the wrong way. To put the little
Mex at his ease, he started to talk after they'd

48

covered a mile.

'What sort of a pilgrim is your boss, Manuelita?'

Orlando stared at the big man and began to relax. That frightening look he'd seen on the big gringo's face as he'd snapped Fallon's arm was completely gone, to be replaced by a lazy grin.

He cleared his throat and said, 'He ... he is a good man, Señor Brazos. Hard perhaps, but fair.'

'Been havin' rustlin' trouble I hear tell?'

'*Sí, sí, mucho trabajo*, much troubles.' Orlando glanced at Fallon's limp form. 'And now the patron has even more trouble.'

'You mean him?' Brazos said, jerking his thumb. 'Heck, that's just one man laid up for a spell, Manuelita. That can't count much on a spread this size.'

'Ah, you do not understand, Señor Brazos. Fallon is the horse breaker on Ranchero Antigua, and there is much work to be done.'

Brazos pulled deeply on his cigarette and smiled to himself as they rode over a low hill and the great ranch house lay before them.

He'd just decided what job he was going to apply for on Rancho Antigua.

FOUR

OLD WHISKY AND YOUNG WOMEN

The sun etched deep pits and hollows in Nathan Kendrick's iron-jawed visage as he stood hatless by the horse corrals watching his men half carry Fallon away to the bunkhouse for repairs.

On the rancher's right, stood the fat Mexican, Pancho Pino, and on his left, his top hand on Rancho Antigua, ramrod Juan Romero.

The three men waited until Fallon was out of sight. The man had been bleating so loud they hadn't been able to hear Orlando when he'd attempted to give an explanation. Now without taking his eyes off Brazos who was sitting his saddle, twisting a cigarette into shape, Kendrick snapped his fingers at his vaquero and Orlando launched into a substantially accurate account of what had taken place out on the trail.

Throughout the story, the three men stood in the sun staring at Brazos, weighing him up with their eyes as he cracked a match on his thumbnail and set fire to his cigarette.

Nathan Kendrick looked the part, Brazos thought. He was big and craggy-faced and looked like it might have been a long time since anybody had ever said no to him. He walked with the aid of a stick, but Brazos couldn't tell if his disability was permanent or temporary. He was dressed in a red and green checked shirt, brown twill trousers and a calf skin vest. He wore no gun and Brazos liked the stamp of the man right from the start.

He wasn't so sure about Juan Romero however, and judging by the ramrod's stormy scowl, it wasn't exactly love at first sight as far as he was concerned either.

Brazos found the Mexican the most colorful and somehow the most interesting of his welcoming committee. Romero was tall for a Mexican, at least six feet one. He carried himself ramrod erect and the broad shoulders and slender hips belonged to a man in perfect physical condition. He was an impressive sight in tight-fitting black trousers flared at the cuffs, white, full-sleeved shirt and a short leather jacket. His long, olive-skinned face was good-looking and strong and there was about the man, an air of pride bordering on arrogance that reminded Brazos a little of the Yank. Juan Romero wore a single bone-handled Colt thonged low on his right hip and it didn't look like an ornament.

'All right,' Nathan Kendrick growled when Orlando was through. 'Now let's hear your story, mister.'

Brazos exhaled a cloud of cigarette smoke and hooked his leg over the saddle pommel.

'Well, it was just about like your man says, Mr. Kendrick. Fallon was ridin' prod. I seen that as soon as he rode up. I tried to talk peaceable to him, but he was just bound and determined to start a ruckus.'

'And you accommodated him?'

'Had no choice, Mr. Kendrick.'

'Did you have to split his face open as well as break his arm?' Romero challenged.

'I only done what I had to do. Like I told him, I didn't ride out here lookin' for trouble, just a job. And that's the way she still stands.' Brazos looked at the rancher. 'What d'you say, Mr. Kendrick?'

Nathan Kendrick didn't say anything for a time, just stood leaning on his walking stick and stroking his big bull jaw. To Romero and the half-dozen homestead hands standing nearby, Kendrick looked his usual tough self, yet underneath the rancher was aware of a faint amusement. He didn't normally find it funny when one of his employees got crippled, but there were extenuating circumstances in this particular case. One was that Lash Fallon was a mean, prickly varmint, long overdue for a thrashing. Another was that for some reason there was something about big Brazos he liked.

'You said you're a horse breaker, mister. You a good one?' Kendrick suddenly said.

'Passable.'

'*Uno momento*, Señor Kendrick,' Romero protested. 'You are not seriously considering hiring this man, are you?'

'Well, we're shy a wrangler, Romero.'

Romero turned his broad back on Brazos and spoke softly to the rancher so the others couldn't overhear. 'Señor Kendrick, I do not like the look of this man. He has the look of a trouble-maker.'

'Well, I don't rightly agree with that. But even if he was, you're an expert at handlin' trouble-makers, ain't you, Romero?'

'I can handle any man, as well you know, patron. But do you not feel that at a time such as this, we have enough problems on the Antigua without adding to them by hiring riff-raff?'

'We need a wrangler,' Kendrick said stubbornly. He wasn't too impressed with his foreman's arguments. Romero was a fine ramrod, but he liked his authority to be undisputed. Big Brazos' handling of Fallon might suggest he wouldn't be an easy man to boss around.

'He might well be a spy for the rustlers,' Romero said, bringing in his last gun. 'How are we to know when a man rides out of nowhere like this?'

'He don't look like no rustler to me,' Kendrick opined, looking at Brazos. 'What he looks like to me is he might be one hell of a good horse-breaker. And seein' as we got horses to break, let's see what he can do.'

Romero shrugged, bowing to his employer's wishes. 'As you wish,' he said stiffly, and turned back to Brazos. 'Very well, señor, we are prepared to give you a trial.' He signaled to the men standing by the corrals. 'Bring out El Fugitivo.'

Brazos swung down, looped the appaloosa's lines over a corral post and pushed his hat onto the back of his head. Judging from Romero's look and the rather surprised expressions on the vaqueros as they hopped off to do his bidding, he was willing to bet a good silver dollar that El Fugitivo was not a lady's hack.

Kendrick and Pancho Pino went across to the corrals and took up vantage points. Men began to appear from all over as the word went around that the big stranger was going to take a crack at El Fugitivo. Brazos hunkered down in the shade of the well and scratched Bullpup's ears. Squatting there, he wasn't sighted by the girl who came down from the house until he spoke.

'Howdy, ma'am.'

The girl stopped and frowned. She was young and dark and wore a white blouse over full breasts, tight-fitting tan riding trousers and hand-tooled Mexican boots. She had a smooth heart-shaped face, a wide, flower-like mouth and long black lashes concealing dark brown eyes that didn't look too friendly as she looked him over.

'Are you the person they're putting on El Fugitivo?'

He got to his feet. 'That's me, ma'am. Hank Brazos. And you'd be Mr. Kendrick's daughter I take it – Orlando mentioned you.'

'I have no wish to know who you are,' she snapped, starting off. Then she paused to say something that explained her antagonism. 'I just saw what you did to Lash Fallon, Mr. Whatever-your-name is. I just hope El Fugitivo does as much damage to you.'

'Always on the cards I guess,' Brazos called after her, but didn't realize how right he might be until the men arrived back with El Fugitivo some minutes later.

Slouching over to the corral fence and building himself a fresh smoke, Brazos ran the quivering, rolling-eyed stallion over with an expert eye. El Fugitivo looked a mean one and no mistake. At least seventeen hands high, he was a blood-red bay, the color the Mexicans call 'Colorado.' He was long-legged, his head small and fine nostrilled, a thick, crested stallion's neck, short back and powerful haunches.

'Never yet has a man ridden El Fugitivo,' runty, rotund little Pancho Pino spoke up at Brazos' shoulder, and Brazos was prepared to believe it. The Mexican went on confidentially, 'You are good horseman are you not, señor? Eef not Pancho Pino would advise you not to be too brave or you may end up dead.'

'Thanks, Pancho,' he grinned. Then the hostlers signaled that the horse was ready. He clambered to the top of the fence, jumped down, then walked across to them, trailing cigarette smoke over his shoulder.

El Fugitivo reared back as Brazos approached, his rolling eyes showing white, whistling and snorting. One vaquero had a tight-handed grip on the head harness at the stallion's underjaw. Another had a fistful of ear, while a worried looking Manuelita Orlando stood by, waiting to help the rider mount.

Brazos paused in front of the stallion and stared him straight in the eye to show he wasn't scared of him. El Fugitivo snorted and stamped his feet, and from the fence Juan Romero called sarcastically:

'This is a new way of breaking a wild horse, caballero?'

Brazos looked over his shoulder, scowled at Romero, then smiled at Kendrick's daughter who just lifted her pretty nose a little higher in the air. Next second he was jumping clear as El Fugitivo jerked his head and savage teeth tore a sleeve clear out of his purple shirt.

'Anxious to get on with it, eh? OK, then.' He pushed Orlando aside, put his foot in the stirrup and swung up. 'Leave him loose!'

The vaqueros let the wild horse go and dashed for the fence. El Fugitivo trembled. He switched his tail once, then exploded around the corral in a dozen enormous straight-ahead bucks that jarred every bone in Hank Brazos' body.

'He is no good, father,' Brenda Kendrick opined over the thump of hoofs and savage snorting as man and horse flashed past. 'He is too big and heavy to be a good wrangler.'

'Well, I don't know,' Kendrick demurred, expert eyes following the action. 'He's still up there.'

A moment later Hank Brazos almost wasn't, as El Fugitivo started whirling in a tight circle with incredible speed, ears laid back, teeth bared.

It was a trick the rider hadn't encountered before, but he hung on. El Fugitivo squealed with rage and lightning fast, whipped his head around and bit a lump out of Brazos' leather chaps. Brazos touched him with the spurs and he tucked his tail, dropped his head and took off again around the corral, pitching and twisting wilder than ever.

It was a ride to remember, and the cowboys cheered themselves hoarse as Brazos rocked in the saddle, loose and relaxed, seeming to anticipate the stallion's every move.

El Fugitivo had plenty of moves. The horse pitched sideways, forward and in circles. He sunfished and he crawfished and every time he came down, it was with four legs as stiff as crowbars, hitting the ground so hard the ground shook far out beyond the corral fence.

For the first minute or so, the cheers were all for El Fugitivo, something of an equine hero on the

Rancho Antigua. But as the contest of man against horse continued some of the applause switched to the rider, until suddenly little Pancho Pino threw his hat in the air and yelled:

'By the Virgin he has done it! He has ridden El Fugitivo!'

The Mexican was premature, but only a little. El Fugitivo still had a few gambits left, and he played them out as hard as he knew how. They didn't come off and the stallion began to slow, then falter, and finally stopped altogether.

It was over.

Brazos patted the trembling neck and swung down. El Fugitivo didn't move. He'd bucked himself to a standstill. He stood with his head down and his forefeet spraddled. He sucked for air in great gasps. His sides heaved like a bellows and sweat coursed in little streams down the insides of his legs, dripping on the sand.

'A good horse with plenty sand,' was Brazos' verdict, and the cowboys cheered wildly.

Brazos went to retrieve his hat, then turned to Kendrick's group. Juan Romero was scowling, Brenda Kendrick had turned away in annoyance, but both Nathan and Pancho were smiling.

'Fine horsemanship, Señor Brazos,' Pino said as he crossed to the fence.

'As good as I've seen,' Kendrick agreed. 'All right Juan, you can fix Brazos up with a feed and a place to sleep. Looks like we got ourselves a new wrangler.'

It was eleven in the morning by the time Benedict had transferred his gear from Arroyo's flea-bag hotel to Garcia's Rooming House. The hotel had been quite impossible and even though the rooming house didn't seem to be much of an improvement, he had been prompted to apply for lodging there after a brief glimpse of a sloe-eyed Mexican girl at the yard pump of the house as he rode slowly by. A minute later he was signing the register under the warming gaze of those same sloe eyes, and displaying his very best smile.

Her name was Jana Garcia. She was the daughter of the proprietress who happened to be absent from Arroyo at the time, leaving Jana in charge. While she made pleasant small talk about the weather, Benedict noted that she was about twenty years of age, a little short of inches in height, but in no other respect. She was quite pretty in a smoldering, earthy way. She had the type of looks that would appeal to some men. Benedict was one of them.

Leaving his black horse in the care of the livery boy at the rooming house, he headed off down the main stem looking for the sheriff. He planned to give Brazos a day to settle in out at the Rancho Antigua, while he himself found out what he could about the spread and the cattle rustling in town before making his appearance at the Rancho.

He found Arroyo's lawman on the front porch of

the jailhouse leaning back leisurely in a cane chair with his spurred boots propped up on the railing. He was a nondescript little man of about fifty with three chins and a calculating eye. He introduced himself as Tom Bindale and shook hands lethargically without getting up. Benedict understood why Gordon had warned him the Arroyo law would be of little help in his investigation. Arroyo was a seedy little town and the sheriff, Tom Bindale, was about the seediest thing he'd encountered in it so far.

But if Bindale was something less than the squared-jaw-of-action type of lawman one might wish for, he was at least able to supply some information when Benedict identified himself and told him what had brought him to his town.

Bindale lost some of his dreamy look and dropped his boot heels to the boards when the matter of the Antigua's rustled stock was raised.

'Mighty peculiar about them there cows you know, Benedict.' He scratched the back of his scalp and spat over the edge of the gallery into the dust. 'You might even say it's kinda spooky.'

Benedict propped a boot up on the porch and leant an elbow on his knee. 'Spooky, Sheriff? How do you mean?'

Bindale spread his hands. 'Why, just the way them beeves seemed to up and disappear. That's what happened to every bunch they've lost over the past couple of months – just vanished! You knew o' course that there's been other rustlin' raids besides the one

Boyd Larsen come to investigate?'

Benedict nodded. Gordon had told him of the previous raids. Apparently Nathan Kendrick had only decided to lodge a claim against the insurance company when the rustlers had finally made a really big strike.

'I know from Larsen's report to head office that he conferred with you about the rustling, Sheriff. Do you have any idea why Larsen was killed?'

'Nary a one. Unless of course he was gettin' too close to the thieves.'

'Do you know a man named Salazar?'

Bindale didn't even bother to conceal his alarm at the mere mention of that name. 'I do, but I wish I didn't, Benedict. That there pilgrim's about the orneriest Mex varmint north of the border. He's wanted all over for just about every crime in the book, but mostly for cuttin' folks' throats.'

Benedict didn't waste time asking what Bindale personally may have ever done to attempt to bring Salazar to justice. Bindale looked as if the limit of his capacity would be to run in a Saturday night drunk. Provided he was very drunk.

He said, 'Have you any idea where this Salazar hangs his hat?'

'Hangs it all over I guess; down in Mexico when he's killin' somebody for money, up in the hills when he's rustlin', west down along the flat country when he takes it in his head to knock over a few stages. But I reckon in between times he does his drinkin' down at Candelaria.'

'Candelaria? That's some miles to the southwest, near the border of the Rancho Antigua, isn't it?'

Bindale nodded and Benedict looked south. It seemed Candelaria might be worth a visit when he was through with Arroyo and Rancho Antigua.

He spent a further half hour with Bindale, fleshing out what he already knew from Henry Gordon and Boyd Larsen's reports. One thing he found significant was that Bindale and Arroyo seemed more puzzled than anything else by the rustling at Rancho Antigua. This stemmed from the fact that the Antigua men, under the leadership of ramrod Juan Romero, had a formidable record against rustlers. Apparently until a few months ago, nobody ever got away with as much as one Antigua cow, then suddenly a hundred cows had vanished, followed by a half-dozen major raids, all of them successful for the rustlers.

Before leaving the lawman to go to lunch, Benedict asked about Keechez, the man referred to briefly in Boyd Larsen's diary as the man who'd given him the information on Bo Rangle. Bindale knew the man. He told him that the Candelaria resident had disappeared, and under prompting, the sheriff recollected he must have vanished just about the same day that Boyd Larsen was killed up in Sabinosa.

Benedict had plenty to occupy his mind as he put himself around a passable steak in the Golden Spoon eatery. Over the meal he made a halfhearted attempt to charm the rather unattractive waitress and engaged a whiskery old bum in conversation. All he gleaned from the girl was that it was singularly pleasant down by the Slave River by moonlight, and from the old barfly that 'Somethin' mighty queer is agoin' on out there at Rancho Antigua.' He paid his own and the old man's tab and went out into the main street again.

With a fresh cigar, he strolled along the shady side of the main stem, considering whether he should ride out to the Antigua that evening or not. He finally decided to wait until next day to give Brazos a chance to settle in out there. As the Reb had not come back to Arroyo yet, it seemed like he'd got the job he went after.

He spent another hour yarning with a clutch of seedy old-timers on the hotel porch, then feeling the need of refreshment, made his way along to the Big Wheel Saloon.

He strolled into the barroom with his customary poise, glancing left and right at the denizens loafing about. The barman, an ugly brute of a man with a cast in one eye, looked over his immaculate figure with surly displeasure. Benedict slapped a hand on the mahogany and smiled.

'A glass of Robbie Burns's whisky, thank you, barkeep.'

The barkeep, a coarse-mannered pig of a man who prided himself as something of a wit, winked heavily at a couple of drinkers nearby, then in a rough but unmistakable mime of Benedict's Harvard tones, replied:

'I am so sorry, but I am regrettably out of Robbie Burns at the moment. Would a glass of Old Ned suit?'

Benedict didn't stop smiling. He was well aware that his appearance and his polished accent often jarred on the ears of hard cases such as this. But he believed dearly in the right of a man to talk and act any way he pleased and never made any attempt to modify his almost foreign sounding speech to conform to the idiom of the frontier. On top of that, he'd taken an instant dislike to the man behind the bar.

'No, I'm very much afraid Old Ned wouldn't suit, fellow,' he smiled, laying the accent on a little heavier still. 'You see, Old Ned is a half-distilled blend of rat poison and swamp water and I strongly suspect that anybody who offers it for public consumption is nothing but a jackass.'

The barman, who had been wiping the bar with a big blue rag, stopped and stared. It took him some time to realize he'd been smilingly insulted. Conscious of the expectant eyes of his admirers upon him, he threw his cloth aside and thrust his belligerent face close to Benedict's.

'Are you lookin' to get that pretty beak of yours busted, panty-waist?'

Benedict was not. What he was actually looking for, was a target for his blurring right elbow. He found it, seemingly by chance in the barman's broad, coarse-pored nose.

Crimson splashed, the barkeep sagged and went white. Before he could gather his senses, Benedict got two handfuls of coarse black hair, then thumped the already squashed nose into the mahogany once or twice and let him go.

The barman disappeared with a crash. Benedict carefully inspected his fingernails. He dearly loved a little violence to keep the appetite sharp, but unless it was completely unavoidable never risked his gun-fighter's valuable hands on hard heads. In the barkeep's case, he hadn't had to.

The Big Wheel was totally silent for a full ten seconds before a rustling and grunting behind the bar revealed that the barman was coming to.

A man sniggered when the battered head finally showed above the level of the mahogany. The man looked as if he'd just lost an argument with a runaway stage.

'Ah there you are, my good fellow,' Benedict said amiably. 'Now shall we try it again? Do you have any Robbie Burns whisky?'

The man blinked his eyes, gasping. 'I . . . I might jest have a bottle in back.'

'Good chap. Well, fetch it if you please. At the double.' The man went down the bar at the double, vanished for a brief moment, then returned at the double, clutching a bottle of Robbie Burns.

Benedict took his drink to a corner table and lit a

fresh cigar. He felt on top of the world; nothing like a little light exercise to sharpen a man up. And there might be something gained by his little dust-up with the barkeep. There were times when stirring things up produced results and he'd well and truly stirred things up here this afternoon.

Later, he joined in a game of poker, lost a few dollars: and kept on with his questioning without learning much that was new. It was approaching dusk when he finally quit the saloon with the intention of heading back for Garcia's Rooming House. It had been a long day, but now it was time for a bath, a change of clothes, another meal at the eatery, and then maybe the luxury of an early night to be fresh for tomorrow.

As he crossed the saloon porch, he saw a fat little Mexican stepping down from a small brown mare at the hitch rack. The horse's rump wore a big scrolled 'A' brand.

Benedict stopped and put on his friendliest smile. 'Buenos noches, Señor.'

The portly little Mexican smiled in cheery response and twisted the reins around the rail. 'A pleasant evening, is it not, Señor?'

'Indeed it is.' Benedict nodded at the horse. 'You're from the Rancho Antigua, amigo?'

'Sí, Señor, I am Pancho Pino, *vaquero*.' Pino looked curiously at the tall gringo. 'Is there something, Señor?'

'Matter of fact there is, amigo. You see, I'm a

stranger in town and could be I'll be looking around for work. I hear that the Antigua is the biggest ranch in a hundred miles. Do you know if they're hiring at the moment?'

Pino shook his head. 'I do not think so, Señor.'

'That's too bad.' Benedict looked at the man keenly. 'They're not hiring anybody, is that it?'

'Well, when you say anybody, Señor . . . just today Señor Kendrick signed on a new horse wrangler . . . but that was only because the job was open and this man rode in asking for work. I do not think . . .'

Pino broke off as the tall American flipped him a silver coin and went down the steps. 'Señor, I do not understand . . .'

'Buy yourself some chilies, amigo,' Benedict called back over his shoulder and was smiling to himself as he strolled down the street. It sounded like Brazos had landed his job on the Antigua; that was encouraging.

Somehow thoughts of stolen cattle, Hank Brazos and early nights vanished the moment he swung through the courtyard gate of the rooming house and saw the girl working the handle of the pump in the yard. It was Jana Garcia, the sloe-eyed daughter of the proprietress who had been friendly and charming when he'd booked in that morning.

He swept off his hat and walked across to her. She was wearing a different dress to the one she'd been wearing when he checked in. It was cleaner, brighter, and there was considerably less of it.

'*Buenos noches*, Señorita Jana.'

'*Buenos noches*, Señor.'

'It is a fine night, is it not?'

The girl looked straight up at the bright yellow moon. She stretched her arms and took a deep breath which probably did Benedict as much good as it did her. 'Si, it is indeed a very fine night.'

'An ideal night for a stroll by the river perhaps?'

'The Señor is bold.'

'The Señorita is beautiful.'

'You really think so, Señor?'

'I am certain of it, Señorita. My arm?'

They passed out through the adobe gateway and strolled arm-in-arm through the quiet street. The night smelt of honeysuckle, roses and sweet grasses. It was spring in Spanish Valley and Benedict decided that for tonight at least, a young man's fancy had no business turning to thoughts of cattle rustlers and dead insurance investigators and unromantic subjects like Bo Rangle . . .

FIVE

RANCHO ANTIGUA

The old sorrel gave Brazos little trouble as he got the speculum fitted into the animal's mouth, but when he suddenly forced the jaws wide open with the spreading device and notched the ratchet to hold them that way, the horse started to panic.

'Hold his head steady, dammit!' he barked to the two Mexican vaqueros.

'He don't like it, Señor Brazos,' Manuelita Orlando observed.

'He don't have to goddam like it. Just hold him.'

'Ees mucho more easy said than done, Señor Brazos,' Pancho Pino chimed in, sweating profusely as he struggled to hold the horse. 'He ees going to keek me if I don' let him go.'

'And I'll keek you if you do, vaquero, and believe me I can keek harder than this old bottle-nose.'

Pancho Pino believed him, so applied himself a little more rigorously to his job and the old sorrel quietened down some.

Brazos went to the fence of the corral and selected the right file from the tool bag. He wiped sweat from his forehead and glanced across at the town trail. No sign of the Yank yet, but he figured it was too early. Benedict kept gambler's hours whenever he could get away with it: late to bed, late to rise, and the hell with health, wealth and wisdom.

As he headed back for the horse, he glanced up at the house and saw Brenda Kendrick standing on the upper gallery. She appeared to be watching him. He gave a friendly wave, but the girl spun on her heel and disappeared.

About to set to work on the old horse again, he looked up at the sound of jingling harness and the clump of hoofs. Ramrod Juan Romero swung down and dropped the lines over a corral post. With athletic ease, the Mexican vaulted the railing, landing inside the corral like a graceful animal. Brazos nodded to him and went on with his task.

'What are you doing?' Romero demanded. 'This horse is finished.'

'Señor Brazos fix the teeths,' supplied Pancho Pino.

'We push open the mouth with the speculum,'

confirmed Orlando. 'We fix the old horse up as good as new.'

'This horse is all through,' Romero repeated, ignoring the expert explanations. 'He's to be shot.'

With the horse's jaws propped open, Brazos ran a finger over the teeth.

'A hell of a lot of hosses don't die of old age,' he commented professionally. 'They croak on account of bad teeth. This here hoss has got plenty of good years left in him yet I figure. All he needs is his teeth filed down even and kept that way so he can chew good and he's liable to live forever and end up an old grey mule.'

Both Pino and Orlando laughed, but Romero was not amused.

'All right,' he said testily, 'get on with it but be quick about it. I have more important jobs for you and these two loafers.'

Brazos shrugged and went on with the job. Romero watched the whole operation closely and when Brazos was through and they'd removed the speculum and released the horse, he said, 'You understand horses, hombre.'

Brazos grunted, dabbing at his face with a bandanna.

'Pack the tools away and put them in the harness shack,' he told the Mexicans. 'Keep the horse corralled and on mash for two days till his teeth stop hurtin'.'

'*Sí*, Señor Brazos.'

'At once, Señor.'

Brazos chuckled. They were a pair of fools right enough, but they were entertaining – and a country mile friendlier than the surly Romero.

And speaking of friendly faces, he suddenly realized another one had shown up.

Brenda Kendrick stood leaning against the gateway with her arms folded and tapping the toe of her riding boot on the hard sand of the yard. She was wearing a yellow blouse, a form-fitting green skirt, a silver comb in her hair and a disapproving expression.

'Mornin', Miss Kendrick.'

The girl ignored his greeting. 'I thought you planned to destroy that horse, Juan?'

'I did,' replied the ramrod.

'Then what is this fellow doing?' She indicated Brazos without looking at him. 'I've been watching from the house. He's wasted an hour fooling with that animal and keeping Pancho and Manuelita from their chores.'

'He says the horse is only suffering from bad teeth.'

'That ees so, Señorita Brenda,' fat Pancho Pino supplied helpfully, returning from the adjoining corral. 'We put the speculum in the mouth and Señor Brazos file all the bad teeth away and . . .'

'Thank you so much, Pancho,' the girl said acidly. 'Now you're both wanted at the house to bring in some cord wood. Pronto.'

'Si, Señorita,' the two men chorused and scuttled for the gateway.

Brazos fingered a packet of Bull Durham from the breast pocket of his purple shirt as he crossed to the fence and leaned against it near where the girl was standing.

He watched her curiously as he built his smoke, then when he had it burning, said quietly,

'You don't like me do you, Miss Kendrick?'

The girl lifted her chin. 'Surely you don't find that surprising?'

'Well, I do in a way. I mean, I couldn't help what happened to Fallon, on account . . .'

'Even without that incident, I'd be opposed to your working on Antigua,' the girl cut in. 'I just don't believe you're the type of man we want working for us.'

Brazos grinned ruefully. 'Well, that's tellin' me I guess.' He exhaled smoke and looked across at Romero. 'But how come you don't like me neither, ramrod? Mebbe what I done to Fallon was a little rich for Miss Kendrick, but you don't strike me as the sensitive kind. What you got against me?'

The girl and Romero exchanged a glance. It was only a glance, yet Brazos sensed something more than that.

Romero's face showed little beyond the respect of an employee towards his boss' daughter, but there was something in the girl's face that went further; something deep and unreadable. Brazos studied the

Mexican ramrod through a haze of cigarette smoke. Yeah, Juan Romero was a pretty impressive-looking joker. He could understand just about any girl finding the ramrod attractive. But the daughter of an American cattle king and a wetback ramrod? No, he had to concede that didn't add up.

The moment was gone and Romero said quietly, 'It is not a matter of like or dislike, cowboy. You were hired against my wishes.'

Brazos frowned. 'But how come, Romero? I'm a good hand with horses.'

'And no doubt you're just as good a hand with your fists and a gun.' Scorn rode the girl's mouth. 'I know your kind only too well, Mr. Brazos, brawling, shiftless . . .'

The girl broke off suddenly at the sound of drumming hoofs. The three turned to see a rider scorching in across the graze from the south-east.

'That's Garcia,' said Romero. 'I sent him out to check the herds on the east graze. Something's wrong!'

Brazos and the ramrod vaulted the corral fence and hurried across to the yard gate together as the lathered rider came drumming up the slope.

'Juan! Juan!' the man was shouting. 'They have struck again! This time the whole herd!'

It took them a minute or more to get the full story from the excited vaquero. He had ridden out to inspect the east herd as instructed, only to find the graze land empty. Thinking the cattle must have broken down the fences, he'd ridden the fence until he'd found where the wires had been cut. He'd followed the tracks for several miles to the Slave River at Sweetwater Basin, found nothing and had then ridden back to the house.

Nathan Kendrick had joined the group around the gate by the time the vaquero was through. The cattle king's face was choleric. 'Three hundred head of my best beeves!' he raged. 'Goddam it all, Romero, what are you waitin' for? Get every man mounted up and get out there. And don't come back without them this time, hear?'

Romero shouted orders, sending men flying off in every direction. Brazos turned to trot towards the porch corrals, but Romero called after him.

'Where are you going, Brazos?'

Brazos stopped. 'Why, to get my hoss, of course.'

'You will remain here at the ranch house,' Romero snapped. 'We do not need you.'

Brazos came tramping back and appealed to Kendrick. 'Look, Mr. Kendrick, I don't know what your ramrod's got agin' me, but I can tell you I take some pride in my sign-readin'. I reckon I could be of plenty help huntin' down them beeves.'

Juan Romero stopped twenty feet away, turned. 'I don't want him with me, Mr. Kendrick,' he said. 'You know why.'

'Romero's got an idea you might be tangled up with the rustlers,' Kendrick explained to Brazos without hesitation. Then he shook his head. 'But I don't figure it that way.' He paused for a moment longer, then said, 'You sure you're a good sign-reader?'

'Tolerable.' Then with a cut at Romero. 'Leastways I reckon I'll tell you where your cattle went, which is more than's happened the last few times by the way I hear it told.'

'All right,' Kendrick decided, 'go saddle up.'

Brazos got his appaloosa and a minute later rode out with Romero at the head of a dozen men. Conscious of the ramrod's eyes upon him, Brazos glanced at him once and if ever he'd seen hate in a man's face, he saw it then. He was puzzled, but didn't dwell on the matter long. He was trying to figure out just what was going on, for he remembered that Benedict had told him that the previously stolen herds from Rancho Antigua had also vanished some-where around Sweetwater Basin.

It was going to be mighty interesting to take a good close look at that basin.

'Who did you say wants to see me?' Nathan Kendrick barked.

'Please, father,' Brenda admonished. 'I'm well aware you have a lot on your mind at the moment, but surely that's no reason to lose your manners.'

Nathan Kendrick stood reproved. Rising from his desk where he'd been going through the dreary routine of calculating what the latest rustling was likely to cost him in hard dollars and cents, he went to his daughter and put his arm around her slim shoulders.

'I'm sorry, honey. Really.'

Her smile was forgiving. 'I understand, father.'

He moved away, slapping at his leg, broken in a riding accident a month ago.

'It's just that I feel so damned useless, Brenda, on account of this. Only for my goddam leg, I could be out with Romero and the boys lookin' for them rustlers.' He turned and looked at her grimly. 'You know somethin', honey?'

'What, father?'

'I got me a powerful hunch this is goin' to be just like before and the times before that as far as my beeves are concerned. I reckon they're goin' to come ridin' back in wore out and empty-handed to tell me they vanished just like the rest did.'

'It's not like you to be discouraged, father.'

Kendrick sighed. 'Mebbe I'm just gettin' old, honey . . . too old.' He frowned in concentration. 'Now who was it you said was waitin' to see me?'

'Mr. Benedict from Southwest Insurance.'

'Benedict? That was the feller Henry Gordon wrote me about, wasn't it?'

'Yes, father.' The girl was smiling and Nathan Kendrick wondered why. 'Shall I show him in, father?'

'Ah, you might as well. Don't feel much like gabbin' to dry-as-dust insurance pilgrims today, but then again, maybe his arrival's timely at that, on

77

account if my hunch about them beeves is right, I'll be filin' claim on his company again, right soon.' He waved a weary hand. 'Bring him in, Brenda.'

Brenda went out. She paused in the hallway to primp at her hair in the mirror, then hurried through to the foyer where the visitor was waiting.

'Ah, Miss Kendrick, is your father ready to see me now?'

Brenda Kendrick felt a stab of annoyance at the way his very voice made her somehow tingle. A young woman as lovely as Brenda in a man's country received more than her share of flattery and attention from every eligible male she encountered, and considered that she'd long since ceased to be impressed by the male species in general, if not in particular. It was a long time, perhaps too long, since a man had excited her on sight, yet that was undoubtedly what had happened to her on the Antigua today. An ordinary morning with more than its ordinary share of problems, and then suddenly this tall, incredibly good-looking man was standing on the stoop with his hat in his hands and smiling at her in a way she hadn't been smiled at in too long, and a voice that established beyond doubt that he was a gentleman.

'Yes,' she replied, trying to be brisk and efficient and sensing she sounded neither. 'Will you come this way, please.'

Kendrick was standing staring broodingly out the window as they entered the study. He turned when

Brenda spoke. 'Father, this is Mr. Benedict from Southwest. Mr. Benedict, my father.'

Kendrick's craggy brows went up in surprise as he shook hands with his visitor. This dapper fellow in the broadcloth suit and the twin, pearl-handled six-guns was hardly what he'd expected stuffy Henry Gordon to send him.

'I'll take your hat, Mr. Benedict,' Brenda offered, and as Benedict turned to the girl with a smile, Nathan Kendrick saw the way she looked at him and understood her smile earlier. Brenda was attracted by the man; he knew her too well not to know the signs. And seeing his daughter in the company of this dashing young man, the cattle baron was suddenly realizing that Brenda didn't get to meet men of this type often enough. He tried to think how long it had been since he'd seen her with any man who could even remotely be termed a suitable prospect for her hand and found he couldn't. Seemed Brenda never even got to town any more, and all there was out here on the Antigua was Mexes, and in Nathan Kendrick's books, they just didn't count.

'I'll make some coffee, father,' Brenda said, and taking Benedict's hat, went out with a smile.

'A very charming girl your daughter, if I may say so, Mr. Kendrick,' Benedict said.

'Reckon she is at that.'

Benedict took his silver cigar case from his pocket. 'A Havana?'

Nathan Kendrick dearly loved a good cigar. He

selected one and Benedict lit it for him, then produced his billfold and extracted his Southwest papers.

'My credentials, Mr. Kendrick.'

Kendrick examined the papers briefly, grunted, then passed them back with a frown.

'Anything wrong, Mr. Kendrick?'

'Not with your papers, Benedict. But seein' 'em just reminded me of the day Larsen came into this very room and showed me his papers just like that.' He shook his big head. 'He was a kinda solemn feller and he drove me loco with all his questions, but I liked him. Hard to believe he was done in.'

'I didn't know him personally, but I believe he was a good man and didn't deserve to get done that way.'

'You Southwest fellers figure him gettin' killed had somethin' to do with what he was workin' on down here?'

'That's how it looks.'

'Hmm,' Kendrick said, looking him up and down again. 'Mebbe now I can understand why they sent a feller like you.'

'How is that, Mr. Kendrick?'

'Well, you dress up kinda flash and you got yourself a fancy Eastern accent there, Benedict, but I got me a feelin' you don't pack them irons of yours just for ornament.' His brows lifted. 'You a gunfighter?'

'No,' Benedict replied truthfully. 'Let's just say I'm a man who doesn't have much stomach for rustling or murder and let it go at that, shall we?'

80

'OK by me. Well, Benedict, did my daughter tell you what happened here last night?'

'No, she didn't.'

'We got hit again.'

'Rustled?'

'Three hundred head of primes. My ramrod and a passel of my boys are out huntin' 'em right this minute, but I got me a sinkin' feelin' in the pit of my stomach they ain't goin' to find 'em.'

Benedict whistled softly through his teeth. 'Three hundred head! It would seem my arrival is rather timely, Mr. Kendrick.'

'Dirty, stinkin' thieves,' Kendrick said bitterly, limping to his desk and flinging himself into his big chair. 'There was a time we wouldn't lose one cow in a whole year, now every goddam time I turn around it seems there's a herd missin'.'

Benedict strolled across the room and dashed his cigar out the open window. He stood there with his brows creased in thought for a moment, then turned to the desk.

'Mr. Kendrick, I rode out to see you this morning to talk over the claims you have made against my company and also to discuss the matter of Boyd Larsen's death. But in view of what you have just told me, I think we should postpone that discussion and concentrate on this latest rustling incident.'

'Suits me,' said Kendrick.

Benedict turned from the windows where he'd been watching vaqueros at work at the corrals.

'Mr. Kendrick, I'd like to inspect the scene of the rustling, and also this Sweetwater Basin. Have you somebody who could show me the way out?'

At that moment light steps sounded in the hallway, the clink of crockery. Benedict went to the door, opened it, and Brenda came in carrying a tray and a silver coffee service. She smiled at Benedict again as she placed the tray on a big oaken table.

'Thanks, honey,' said Kendrick. 'Say, are any of the house boys still around?'

'Why no, father, you sent them all out with Juan. Why?'

'Well, Mr. Benedict wanted to ride out to the basin and take a look around, but it looks as if he'll have to wait until some of the boys come in from the range. That is, unless you're a good trailsman, Mr. Benedict? If you are, I could give you directions how to . . .'

'I think I'd prefer somebody to show me around, Mr. Kendrick.'

'I could show you the way, Mr. Benedict.'

Both men looked at the girl. Kendrick suddenly grinned. 'Why hell, of course she could, Benedict. Nobody knows the Antigua better than Brenda. And besides, it'll do you good, honey. You've been around the house too much lately and lookin' kinda peaked I've noticed.'

If Kendrick expected to get any argument about his choice of guide from Benedict, he was as wrong as he could be. 'Why, that's more than kind of you,

Miss Brenda. I hope it's not an inconvenience to you.'

'Not at all,' the girl assured him, and her father was astonished to see the hint of color in her cheeks as she headed for the door. 'I'll saddle my horse and meet you out front in five minutes.'

'Takes about an hour to get out to the basin from here,' Kendrick explained. He limped across to the big front window and beckoned Benedict across. He pointed southeast to where a jagged ridge of mountains chopped into the brassy New Mexico sky. 'Them ridges are the Bucksaws. They border the basin on the south side. The basin itself is about eight miles long, best grazin' land on the Antigua. The Slave River runs right through the basin – you know, the same river that winds around Arroyo?'

Benedict knew that particular stretch of river quite well, having spent half the previous moonlight night on its lush green banks at Arroyo.

'Do you have any theories on how your cattle might have disappeared, Mr. Kendrick?'

'Make that Nathan. No, Benedict, it's a mystery to me. Of course when any stock disappears in these parts, you immediately think about the badlands that lie south of the Bucksaws and stretch all the way across the Mexican border. But I've had Romero and the boys go over that country a dozen times and they ain't found hide nor hair of a track.'

'I was talking to Sheriff Bindale and others in town yesterday, Nathan. The general idea seems to be that the cattle you've lost just seem to have been, well, swallowed up. Surely this is not the case?'

Nathan Kendrick scowled mightily. 'I know it sounds crazy, even to me, but that's just about the size of it.' He brightened a little. 'Anyway, you seem a tolerably smart young feller. Maybe you can come up with somethin'.'

'Let's hope so. You say all your men went out with your ramrod?'

'Yeah.'

'You employ expert sign-readers of course?'

'Well, I figured they were expert until I started losin' beeves. But we got a new hand just signed on ridin' with Romero today. Says he's good. Mebbe he'll bring 'em some luck.'

Benedict nodded to himself. That's what he'd been fishing to find out. If Brazos was out there, then the best sign-reader he'd ever struck was hunting Antigua's stolen stock.

There was a short silence, then Kendrick said abruptly, 'Are you married, Benedict?'

Benedict looked at the older man in surprise. 'Married? Why . . . why no, I'm not. But why do you ask?'

'Oh I guess I'm just a curious old cuss by nature,' Kendrick said easily. 'Always like to find out as much about folks I come into contact with as I can.' He stared out the window again. 'Well, there's Brenda comin' up with her paint. You'd better get out there pronto as she ain't exactly a patient gal.' He chuckled.

'Kinda like me in that way, I guess.'

Benedict crossed the room, paused with his hand on the porcelain knob. 'What time do you want her home, Nathan?'

'Well, I don't like her out on the range late. Anyway, there's cloud buildin' up from the south. Looks like there won't be no moon tonight so I reckon you'll all be comin' in at dark. So that'll do.' He touched his hand to his forehead. 'Best of luck, Benedict.'

Benedict nodded and went out. He picked up his hat from the hallstand and walked through to the front yard. Brenda was sitting her little paint pony near the hitch rack where his black horse was tied. From the big window Kendrick watched them mount up. The two exchanged smiles, then rode off side by side out through the big gate and headed across the rangeland.

The cattle king stroked his bull jaw and nodded thoughtfully to himself, watching them go. In one way he hoped Benedict might get to the bottom of things quickly, but on the other hand it mightn't be such a bad thing if the fellow was obliged to hang around for a spell.

He hadn't seen his daughter in such agreeable spirits in longer than he cared to remember.

SIX

THE VANISHING HERD

Romero threw the dregs of his coffee on the fire.

'All right, let us get on with it.'

The horsemen were weary after six solid hours in the saddle, but there was no argument. To the simple men of Rancho Antigua, Nathan Kendrick was God and Juan Romero was His deputy.

The towering ramparts of the Bucksaws were throwing huge shadows across Slave River and Sweetwater Basin as the riders swung up. A vaquero emptied the coffee pot over the little fire they'd built on the river bluffs, then stamped out the ashes. Clouds were banking up over the badlands and creeping slowly across the sky towards the afternoon sun.

'I theenk I have blisters on my backside for a month,' lamented Pancho Pino who was strictly a homestead vaquero.

'You have blisters?' said self-pitying Manuelita Orlando, another bunkhouse cowboy. 'By the Blessed Virgin of Guadeloupe, I have blisters on my blisters.'

'One theeng is good,' Pino comforted them both as the cavalcade got under way. 'See how the clouds come. A leetle while back I hear Señor Brazos remark that we will be unable to follow the sign tonight.'

'Does that mean that we go back to the ranchero?'

'Perhaps.' Pino frowned back over his shoulder. 'Ay, look, he does not come weeth us.'

The two men reined in and looked back. Hank Brazos, who hadn't taken the ten-minute break for coffee, was still walking up and down examining the prints of the rustled cattle, where they'd come out of the river, for about the twentieth time.

Some distance ahead, Juan Romero swore as he turned and saw the two men halted, and only then spotted Brazos farther back.

'Hold hard!' he shouted to his riders, then cantering back a short distance, yelled: 'Hey, cowboy!'

Brazos looked up but made no move to mount up. His horse stood under a tree and Bullpup had gone to sleep beneath him.

Romero swore in Spanish and heeled back down to the river, jerking his horse to a tail-sitting stop.

'What do you think you are doing, hombre?'

'Readin' sign.'

'Then might I point out to you that the sign leads east as any man with half an eye could see.'

'Oh, ain't no doubt at all about that,' Brazos agreed with a puzzled frown that had not been absent from his face for the past twenty minutes. 'But there's somethin' wrong with this here sign, Romero.'

'There is?' Romero's tone was sarcastic. 'Then perhaps you can explain what it is.'

Brazos could, but he just wasn't ready to do so quite yet. Turning his back on the straw boss, he walked slowly back down towards the water. Underfoot were the deep plowed tracks of many hoofs in the soft riverbank earth leading out of the water. Many times in the eight miles that they'd followed the Slave from the western end of Sweetwater Basin to where he stood now at the eastern end, the tracks of the cattle had disappeared into the river, then reappeared again farther on. It was an old rustling trick to confuse the pursuit and it had successfully delayed them many hours during the day.

But now there was something amiss with the tracks, leastways he was pretty sure there was.

He turned his head as Romero dismounted and strode down the slope, the ramrod's face pale and tight in the shadowy gloom of the towering cliffs.

'Figured it out for yourself yet, Romero?' he asked, disarming the Mexican's annoyance a little with a crooked grin.

'I have figured nothing out,' Romero replied tightly, 'because there is nothing to figure out. Now . . .'

'How many beeves you reckon made these tracks we're standin' on?'

'What sort of a question is that? Three hundred of course.'

Brazos shook his head slowly. 'Wrong. More like a hundred and fifty. Mebbe even less than that.'

'What nonsense is this? Were not three hundred head stolen? And have we not been following the same set of tracks all day long?'

'We were followin' that many.' Brazos gestured at the river. 'Seems to me they drove three hundred head in up there, but only a hundred and fifty odd come out down here.'

Romero sneered. 'Impossible.'

'Mebbe so, but that's how I read it.'

'We shall soon see if what you say is so.' The ramrod turned and whistled through his teeth at the vaqueros. 'Miguel,' he shouted, 'come down here.'

Miguel Chaves, the Antigua's top sign-reader, detached himself from the bunch and rode back.

Romero said, 'Examine this sign and tell me how many cattle came out of the river here, Miguel.'

Chaves swung down and inspected the hoof-torn earth. He straightened and said, 'The full herd, Juan. Three hundred beeves. But how could it be other-wise?'

'Never mind that,' Romero said. He turned to Brazos with a crooked smile. 'Well, Señor?'

Brazos said nothing, but he was thinking plenty. Not only was there a mystery about the tracks, now there was a mystery about Miguel Chaves. The man had read the sign wrong.

'Very well, enough is enough,' Romero snapped. 'You will either mount up and ride with the rest of us immediately or you can return to the house and inform Señor Kendrick that I have no further use for you.'

With that Romero spun on his heel, strode back to his horse and rode off. Brazos stood frowning down at the tracks for another handful of seconds, then slouched across to the appaloosa and filled leather.

He rode a little distance then reined in, looking back. He was reluctant to leave Sweetwater Basin, for this was the area where all the rustled cows had disappeared.

Yet there was nothing to be found in the basin and he knew it as well as anybody else having already combed its length. The beautiful basin, shaped roughly like a bottle, was a smooth, gently undulating expanse of rangeland bordered by low hills to the north and by the inaccessible, glass-smooth ramparts of the Bucksaw cliffs to the south. The Slave hugged the base of those cliffs for most of its journey through the basin and the few patches of graze on the southern banks between the water and the cliff base couldn't conceal a flock of chickens let alone three hundred head of beeves.

Romero shouted to him again and reluctantly he turned his broad and muscular back on the basin, touched the appaloosa with his heels and rode up to join them.

They followed the tracks for a further hour. It was easy going. The rustlers had made no attempt to conceal the sign here, nor had they made any further attempt to point the cattle back to the river.

It was Romero himself who spotted the first beef. The animal was standing looking pretty beat and bleary-eyed by the lip of an arroyo chomping on gamma grass.

The riders inspected the beef curiously, then pressed on. A whoop of triumph went up from one of the lead vaqueros as he reached the rim of the arroyo and saw below him, dotted across the floor of the arroyo, peacefully munching grass, the rest of the herd.

Or so they believed until Brazos reined up on the arroyo edge and took a look. And what he saw gave him some satisfaction, even if it did at the same time confuse him far more than he'd been confused before.

'There's not three hundred head of beeves there,' he told Romero. 'A hundred and twenty at the most.'

Romero didn't believe him at first, or seemed not to. But a quick count quickly proved Brazos right. The herd in the arroyo tallied one hundred and seventeen head and not one more.

There was an obvious explanation for that, Romero was quick to point out. This was only part of the herd. The rest had been driven on farther.

That theory held water until the cowboys had scouted around the entire perimeter of the arroyo and found not a solitary track leading out.

They were still puzzling over the mystery, Brazos as deeply as anybody, when they were hailed from behind. He turned in the saddle to see Benedict riding in with Brenda Kendrick.

Brazos grinned to himself as he watched Romero, hard-eyed, ride out to meet the pair. He didn't know how Benedict managed it, but he always seemed to turn up with a good-looking woman.

'This is Mr. Duke Benedict of Southwest Insurance, Juan,' Brenda Kendrick said as Romero reined in before them. 'Have you had any luck with the cattle?'

Romero studied Benedict for a silent moment before answering.

'We have recovered half the herd, but the rest, they have just vanished.'

'Vanished, Romero?' said Benedict. 'The way those other beeves vanished?'

'It would seem so.'

Benedict frowned and looked back the way they'd come. 'You mean they disappeared somewhere along the basin?'

'Yes.'

'But how? Brenda and I followed your tracks along

the river. I didn't see anything along the cliffs other than a few caves. There were no canyons or passes that cattle could be driven through.'

'That's right, Juan,' said the girl. 'How could the cattle possibly disappear in the basin?'

'I do not know.'

Benedict questioned Romero for some time, but the ramrod was unable to shed any further light on the mystery of the vanishing herd. Then the cowboys approached driving the remainder of the cattle and Romero said,

'It is time to return to the homestead. We can talk further this evening if you wish, Señor Benedict.'

Benedict nodded in silent agreement, a puzzled frown creasing his brows. As they fell in with the herd, he saw Brazos riding slouched in the saddle flicking little river pebbles down to bounce off Bullpup's iron skull. Their glances met briefly and Brazos gave an imperceptible shrug to suggest he was as much in the dark as everybody else.

Duke Benedict was pensive and thoughtful as he lit an expensive cigar. If Brazos hadn't been able to figure out what had happened from the sign, then they had a real mystery on their hands.

They crossed the river and followed the herd down Sweetwater Basin. The dull thudding of the hoofs bounced off the ancient stones, the river growled deep in its bottom. The sun rapidly lost territory in the western sky as they rode, finally sinking in a spectacular burst of gold and crimson.

Benedict and Brazos rode level on opposite sides of the herd about a hundred yards behind Juan Romero and Brenda Kendrick. And despite his concentration on the empty walls of the basin, Brazos couldn't help noticing how the girl frequently turned in the saddle to look back at Benedict.

Juan Romero noticed it too.

SEVEN

BO RANGLE'S WAY

The door opened and Slim Samson came in looking tense.

'Bo, Arrillaga's just rode into town. He's got Drago and about a dozen of his hard cases with him.'

The man who turned from the broken window of the hovel on the edge of Mescalero was about thirty, but appeared much older because of the treachery asleep in his green eyes and the etched lines of cruelty cutting the corners of his mouth. His hat lay carelessly on the extreme back edge of coarse black hair that grew like a mane and was chopped off square at the shirt collar. He was tall, with a narrow, flat middle, heavy sloping shoulders, and a deep voice that, even when he spoke softly, trembled the dust motes in the still air of the room.

'Relax, Slim, no need to get all in a twist. We're

just goin' to parley with him.'

'I got me a hunch he means to try and beat us down on price, Bo.'

Rangle crossed the room. He walked like a man with more savage energy than he could ever burn up.

'That's on the cards. Our companero Arrillaga knows we're relyin' on him to take the Antigua beeves off our hands, so he'll mebbe try offerin' us even less than he did last night.'

'But hell, Bo, that ain't no good. We took plenty risks liftin' that herd we got out on the flats. Five dollars is lousy enough, but any less and it ain't worth the trouble stealin' 'em.'

'You worry too much. He needs us as much as we need him. C'mon, let's go see Señor Arrillaga and find out where he stands first.'

They quit the room and headed up the street for Lobato's cantina where a bunch of Mexican ponies were racked out front. Slim Samson was forced to half-trot to keep up with Rangle's lunging strides.

Bo Rangle's expression was pensive as he walked thinking about Arrillaga. When Rangle had first come in on the Antigua rustling deal, Lobato the saloonkeeper had been agent for the stolen beeves. When Arrillaga had moved in and shouldered Lobato out, Rangle hadn't cared one way or the other. Now Arrillaga was getting greedy – and that was different.

They found Virgil Arrillaga seated at a table with his back to the wall in the cantina, flanked by scummy-looking Mexes weighed down with big rusty guns, and enough knives to open a cutlery business. Drago, Arrillaga's beanpole, hawk-faced bodyguard, stood by the bar with his evil, muddy-colored eyes flickering around like a dangerous dog. Lobato, the cantina owner with ambition, was behind the bar with his hands out of sight. Some ten or twelve hard-looking local riff-raff were seated about drinking tequila and saying nothing.

Bo Rangle walked directly up to Arrillaga's table and grinned.

'Right on time, Virgil.'

'Ah, my companero, Bo,' the Mexican said expansively. 'Drago, fetch a glass of good wine for Señor Rangle.' He pulled out a chair. 'Come, my friend, be seated and let us discuss our affairs like gentlemen in comfort.'

Everybody relaxed as Rangle sat down, grinning, as friendly as hell. Last night when Arrillaga and Rangle had failed to come to terms on a price for the stolen stock, Bo Rangle had left in an angry mood, but tonight he was a different man.

'To your very good health, Virgil,' Rangle said when the scowling Drago fetched his drink.

'And to good business,' Arrillaga responded, lifting his glass. He took a sip of his wine, then said, 'Well, Bo, you have considered my offer?'

'Sure have.'

'And?'

'Well, you said you might come up with a new

price by tonight, Virgil. Let's have it.'

Arrillaga smiled like a big ugly cat. He was half-Mex, part Apache with a dash of Negro and a touch of Chinese. He was a man of various talents, all of them bad.

'Three dollars a head.'

Bo Rangle nodded his head and smiled. Yesterday it had been five bucks. The beeves were worth at least twenty.

'OK, Arrillaga, you're the boss.'

Arrillaga's smile spread ear-to-ear as he looked across at Drago. He fished out a roll of greasy bills, and for a moment every hungry eye in the cantina was focused on more money than most of them would earn in a lifetime.

In that moment Rangle moved with the ferocious speed of an attacking jaguar. A knife flashed as he leapt behind Arrillaga, clutched him over the face with his left hand, reefed his head back with a savage wrench and put the first tenth of an inch of the steel in his drum-taut neck.

Nobody moved. Nobody breathed.

'All right,' Rangle hissed, 'tell 'em to shuck their guns.'

Arrillaga didn't cry out in terror or rage. His body was flaccid in Rangle's iron grip. His yellow face was stretched into hideous distortion. A rivulet of vivid red blood ran slowly down his stretched neck, his eyes bulging.

He could hardly whisper. 'Thees one beeg

mistake, my frien'. But do as he say.'

The men hesitated, but only until Lobato came up with his shotgun.

'You heard him, companeros!'

It was the signal for Lobato's men to haul iron and get to their feet and a gaping Slim Samson realized that Bo and Lobato had planned the whole thing.

Unsteady fingers tugged out six-guns and dropped them noisily to the floor. Drago hesitated, his muddy eyes blazing with a rage that shook his lean frame head to foot.

'Tell him,' Bo Rangle whispered in Arrillaga's ear, the bass voice vibrating. 'Tell him to get shook of his gun or I'll kill you.'

Arrillaga licked ashen lips with a pointed pink tongue, his face now sheened with sickly sweat.

'Do as he says, Drago.'

Drago twitched with venom, but pulled his gun and placed it on the bar. Bo Rangle, with a devil's grin, rammed his knee in Arrillaga's back and cut Arrillaga's tight, yellow throat right across and all the way to the bone.

Arrillaga got off just one scream as the vivid stream of life gushed forth. Rangle snaked the man's gun from his holster, let the twitching body flop down, and shot Drago straight between the eyes.

The cantina went still as a morgue as Drago's body stopped twitching. His face wearing a savage look that Samson knew only too well, Bo Rangle waved his smoking gun.

'OK, gents, let's parley.' The gun froze on a hulking badman with walrus moustaches like a bull's horns. 'Sanchez, I guess you're number one now Virgil and Drago have kind of resigned.'

The big man licked dry lips and nodded. 'Si . . . I suppose that is so.'

'Right, then this is the new deal. You, Lobato and me, we all work in together. I steal the beeves, you sell 'em in Mexico and Lobato does the organisin' here like he done afore Arrillaga horned in. Lobato gets a ten per cent cut off top and I get fifty. That's sixty per cent, and you get the rest. How's that hit you, companero?'

Sanchez looked at Arrillaga. Then he looked at Drago. Finally his calculating eye came to rest on Bo Rangle and there was only one answer a sane man could give.

'I theenk we work well together, Señor Rangle. It is as you say, a deal.'

'Figured you'd see things my way,' Rangle said and winked at a relieved Samson. He picked up Arrillaga's blood-stained roll and stepped over the corpse and went to the bar. 'OK, get rid of the dead meat, and let's have a drink. Come on, Lobato, look sharp, this is a big day.'

Lobato laughed to relieve his own tension and reached for a bottle of his best.

'We did it, companero!' he exulted. 'We did it!'

'Sure, sure. But now you're back in the box seat here, I expect you to handle your end right, fat boy.'

'Of course, you can rely on Lobato. There will be as you say, many more cattle?'

'Any amount.'

'All from Rancho Antigua?'

'Keerect.'

'When can we expect the next delivery?'

'Well, now we've straightened things out here, I'll be pullin' out for the north at first light. A day's hard ridin'll get me there. The beeves will be waitin' for me, so I'll be headin' straight back. I guess about next Wednesday you can start lookin' for us.'

'You say the cattle will be waiting? You mean they've already been stolen?'

'Dead right eh, Slim?'

Samson nodded at Rangle's elbow. 'Right sure enough, Bo. We're what you call organized, Lobato.'

Lobato smiled in wonderment at gringo efficiency, then stopped smiling when he got a look at Arrillaga's throat as they packed him out. A tremor of apprehension went over the man as he looked sideways at his new 'partner' who was whistling a tune in perfect time to the lolling of Arrillaga's almost severed head.

Lobato poured himself a treble tequila.

On the day following the rustling at the east graze, Duke Benedict came out to Rancho Antigua to take another look around. Nathan Kendrick gave him permission to borrow Hank Brazos when Benedict told him he'd been impressed by the man's sign-reading ability, and the two spent the day going over the east graze, Sweetwater Basin, the Slave River, and the arroyo where some of the beeves had been recovered.

They found nothing.

That night, Kendrick invited the 'insurance man' to dine with them at the great house. Kendrick still liked the idea of Brenda and Benedict, and was pleased to see them getting along so well together. But he was in a heavy mood that evening despite Benedict's entertaining conversation. He was deeply concerned about the latest attack on his herds.

Juan Romero was deeply concerned as well, or at least the ramrod who'd been invited to dine with them, was in a heavier mood than Kendrick had ever seen him. Romero barely spoke during the long meal, and later when Brenda played the piano and sang for them, he just stood by the hearth with his arms folded, his eyes flicking from Brenda to Benedict and speaking only when spoken to.

It wasn't until after Benedict had entertained them with a completely professional rendition of Lincoln's Gettysburg Address and a maid-servant brought in coffee, that Kendrick guided the conversation back to what they'd been discussing over the meal and asked Benedict what he planned to do next.

'Well, I haven't quite decided,' Benedict said, standing by the great marble hearth, coffee cup in hand. 'So far, I haven't come up with a great deal that means anything. I'm wondering if you gentlemen know of anything I might have overlooked, something that could possibly give me the lead I'm searching for.'

Kendrick sighed. 'Well, Benedict, I'm afraid I've told you all I can. What about you, Juan?'

'I too can add nothing to what Señor Benedict already knows,' said the ramrod.

Benedict said, 'In the short time I've been here, Romero, I've seen enough to know that you're a very proficient ranch foreman, with your finger on the pulse of everything that goes on here at Antigua. Are you sure you haven't seen or heard something that might offer just one clue as to how these cattle have simply vanished?'

The Mexican foreman shook his dark head.

'I have puzzled over the matter until my head aches, Señor. With my men I have combed every inch of the ranchero, but each time it is the same. Nothing.'

Benedict sighed.

'Well in that case, I suppose I might as well concentrate my attention on the one slender lead I had when I left Summit.'

'What is that, Duke?' Brenda asked.

'This man Salazar, the man who killed Boyd Larsen. It seems reasonable to assume Salazar is connected with the rustlers, and I have learned that the man frequents Candelaria from time to time. I shall most likely visit there tomorrow and take a look around.'

'Might lead to somethin',' Kendrick agreed. 'It's a real pest-hole that place.'

'It's also a very dangerous place I believe, Duke,' warned Brenda, lovely in a floor-sweeping black gown cut daringly low at the bodice. 'It's a Mexican town and the only Americans you'll find there are badmen or drunks. You'll have to be very careful.'

'Don't worry, I intend to be, Brenda.'

It was some time after that the silent Juan Romero excused himself briefly and left the room. On the front gallery, the ramrod paused in the brilliant moonlight, his eyes playing over the headquarters. It was after eleven and all was still. A dim light burned in the stables and from far to the east came the solitary sound of a coyote.

The ramrod's face was pale in the silvery light as he went down the wide stone steps and headed for his room which jutted off the north end of the main bunkhouse. As he walked, he glanced up several times at the wooded knoll that lay a mile to the north of the ranch house above the trail to town. He went quietly up the steps, opened the door and disappeared inside.

Something moved in the black shadows of the main barn fifty yards down the slope. A cigarette end burned red and threw a brief glow over Hank Brazos' face as he drew deep.

The blue eyes watched Romero's room. The light went on, dim behind the curtains. Then the curtains were opened for several seconds, closed, opened again, then closed a final time.

The window went dark. Brazos shielded his cigarette in his hand and moved back deeper into the shadows as the door opened. Romero stood on the stoop, his head turning from side to side as he looked about him, then went quickly up the moonlit yard and disappeared back into the house.

Brazos came slowly out of the shadows, shoulders looking enormous in the moonlight. His saddle brown face wore an expression that was almost painful, but which only signified that he was puzzled. After some time he resumed the restless prowling about that had been interrupted at Romero's appearance. He never could sleep when he had something on his mind. And now he had even more to puzzle him than before.

Somewhere deep in the great house, a clock tolled the solemn hour of midnight.

Benedict rose to take his leave. 'A most pleasant evening, Nathan.' A handsome smile for Brenda. 'And very pleasant company.' He nodded to solemn Romero. 'Cheer up, Juan, we'll get to the bottom of this rustling business yet.'

'Best of luck in Candelaria,' said Romero.

'Brenda will show you out, Benedict,' Kendrick said. 'I got to rest this leg of mine. Juan, you stay on a minute, will you? I want to talk to you about that sick bull.'

Benedict was frowning thoughtfully as they crossed the moon-washed gallery to stand at the top of the steps.

'Romero seems to be in a surly mood tonight, Brenda,' he said, looking back along the hallway. 'You any idea why?'

The girl turned her face away.

'Juan has a lot on his mind at the moment, that is all. He . . . he feels badly about the loss of the cattle.'

'Yes, I suppose he would at that.' He took her hand. 'Well, Brenda, thanks again for a charming evening.'

He kissed her hand and their eyes met and locked. Benedict began to draw her towards him. She resisted, but not convincingly. He knew he was acting rashly, that tough old Kendrick would likely toss him off Antigua and have him fired from Southwest, if he thought he had designs on his daughter. But he'd never considered the consequences where a woman was concerned before and he wasn't about to start now.

Brenda suddenly pulled away at a sound from inside. It was only a door opening, but it broke the spell.

'Good night, Duke,' she whispered and ran inside.

Benedict smiled ruefully and felt for a Havana. Maybe it was just as well, he philosophized, heading for the stables. He had enough to occupy him at the moment without the threat of Kendrick coming looking for him with a bullwhip. Even so, it was hard to get her out of his mind, that expensive womanly smell, the intelligent brilliance of lovely brown eyes . . .

The stables were dim. He turned up the night light, then came whirling around in a lightning twist with a six-gun in his fist at the sound of a step.

Brazos grinned as he emerged from a stall, chewing a straw.

'Well, one thing, Yank, you ain't slowin' up none.'

Benedict looked annoyed as he put away the gun that had come out as fast, and maybe faster, than Hank Brazos had ever seen a man draw.

'That's one way of dying young,' he snapped. 'What the devil are you doing, skulking about anyway?'

Brazos leant his shoulder against a stanchion, big hands hooked in his shell belt.

'Couldn't sleep.'

'Is that any reason for giving a man a start like that?'

'Never meant to. I was just hangin' about in here so's nobody'd see me talking to you.'

Swinging his saddle onto his black, Benedict said, 'What's on your mind?'

'I ain't dead sure,' Brazos rubbed his rock of a jaw. 'Say, Yank, what do you make of Romero?'

'Why . . . why he's moody, proud I guess, and from all reports, a good ramrod. Why?'

'Somethin' not right about that joker.' He told Benedict what he'd witnessed an hour back. 'What do you make of that, Yank?'

Duke Benedict wasn't sure. The window business sounded like some sort of a signal. But why would

Romero want to be signaling in the middle of the night? And to whom?

'Maybe it's just something to do with the sentries,' he decided, swinging up.

'Could be, but I got a kind of hunch somethin's cookin'. Better keep sharp.'

'I always keep sharp. Well, I'll be seeing you in a few days, Reb. You can reach me in Candelaria if anything breaks.'

Brazos just grunted, and Benedict rode out, leaving him standing there, still leaning against the post. The hoofs of the horse beat loud in the midnight stillness, as he crossed the yard, passed through the gate, then cantered along the trail.

He didn't put too much store by Brazos' warning, as the Reb got more hunches than a Gila monster got flies. Even so, he did keep sharp.

And it was only because he was doubly vigilant, that he saw the flicker of movement in the high rocks over the trail as he rode up the first hill. It wasn't much – just something moving up there that could have been a badger foraging or the breeze stirring a shrub.

Only it was the wrong kind of terrain for badgers and the night was as still as a grave.

Benedict fisted a gun, slewed his horse suddenly off the trail and spurred him up the steep slope that led to the crest. He heard a startled gasp, glimpsed the moving shape of a sombrero, then ducked as moonlight starred on steel.

Something hummed overhead like a deadly insect. He thought it was a bullet, but there was no crash of a shot, no blossom of gun flame. He shot a glance behind him as he flung from the saddle and saw the throwing knife strike sparks from a stone, kick left and bounce down the steep drop to the trail. A gun in each hand then, he sped up the ridge in a crouch.

Reaching the nest of rocks where the ambusher had waited, he glimpsed a fast shadow disappearing into a second, isolated cluster of tumbled stones thirty feet away. Benedict squeezed off a shot and was rewarded by a cry of pain, then gun flame blossoming like some vivid desert flower in the gloom as the drygulcher answered back.

Benedict crouched behind a boulder to reload. He stayed down as bullets smashed against the stones, then he heard a hammer click on an empty. He bobbed up and drove two deadly accurate shots into the rocks.

He waited.

The drygulcher was just as patient as he, but not as smart. A full minute passed, and then drifting up from the ranch house came the sound of galloping hoofs.

A muffled curse came from the Mexican's position. He hadn't selected the ridge from the point of view of defense, but only for attack. Open land stretched away on all sides of his rock nest – save for the side where Benedict was waiting.

Suddenly he burst from cover with explosive

speed. A gun flared in the charging man's hand and Benedict threw himself violently aside as lead screamed almost too close. Benedict triggered, the figure lurched and screamed, caught his balance and hurled himself over Benedict's rock, with a mad-dog snarl.

Rearing back, Benedict let him have both barrels. The ambusher's momentum kept him sailing clean overhead, and Benedict recognized the savage face just before he turned over in the air, hit an outcrop of stone hard on the way down, then pitched onto the trail.

Salazar.

EIGHT

FIRE IN THE BLOOD

Benedict was in no hurry to move. That had been damned close. Still sprawled on the stones, he reloaded his guns and turned his head as Juan Romero and Hank Brazos came galloping up the rise in the trail with more horsemen straggling out from the headquarters behind.

Romero reached the dead man first. He swung down, turned him over on his back, and in the brilliant moonlight, the watching Benedict clearly saw his expression of shocked disbelief.

Brazos went up to meet Benedict as he climbed down to the trail.

'Goddamit, Yank, I always said you was harder to kill than a rattler.' He said softly, 'What happened? This greaser son-of-a-bitch try to jump you?'

Benedict nodded, watching Romero below. 'That's

right. You recognize him of course?'

Brazos gave the bullet-shattered body a contemptuous glance. 'Sure, it's Salazar. What do you make of it, Yank?'

Duke Benedict wasn't sure what he made of it. Then he had a thought. Salazar likely had a horse cached close by. Maybe if he could find the horse and backtrack Salazar, he might learn where he'd come from, which could be the first step towards learning why he'd come.

'I'll keep in touch,' he said before heading for his horse. 'And you'd better sleep with one eye open until you hear from me.'

Brazos grunted and walked back down the hill to join Romero as Benedict swung up and rode over the crest of the ridge. He rode directly to a stand of elms two hundred yards west of the ridge-top in a grassy hollow. It was the obvious place to cache a horse, and sure enough there was a saddled mustang there, tethered to a tree.

He set the animal loose, then followed the sign Salazar had made coming in. He was no tracker, but a child could have followed the clear hoof prints under the brilliant moonlight. Salazar obviously hadn't been worried about being pursued after finishing his job.

His thoughts focused on Juan Romero as he followed the sign swiftly through the low hills, with cattle looking stupidly after him. The suspicion was hard in his mind that Romero had been signaling up to the waiting Salazar earlier. And Brazos was plainly doubtful about the man – yet it still didn't add up. Romero was a clever man with a well-paid and responsible job on Rancho Antigua and years of devoted service to Kendrick behind him. What could he possibly have to do with either Salazar or the mystery that hung over Rancho Antigua? It didn't even begin to make sense, and he was forced to the conclusion that there were unknown, but innocent reasons behind the ramrod's animosity towards he and Brazos.

He estimated he'd ridden some five miles by the time the tracks led him to a timbered draw, where a horse whinnied at his approach. Using spurs, he put the black to a zigzagging gallop and crouched in the saddle. He reached the trees without drawing fire. He swung down, and with Colts drawn, waited.

'Pancho! Is that you?'

Benedict's eyes widened fractionally. A woman's voice. 'Pancho?'

He moved stealthily towards the voice. He came to a clearing where a saddled pony stood with pricked ears. Moving a little closer, he saw the girl standing with her back to him. He lowered his guns and stepped from the trees.

'*Buenos noches*, Señorita.'

She spun with a startled cry and a spill of raven hair. Her eyes were black pools of animal alertness as she stared at him.

'Who are you?' Her voice was a whisper.

'Well, I'm not Salazar.'

The brief fear was gone from her face to be replaced by something dangerous as she moved slowly towards him.

'You . . . you are the hombre he was to kill?' Her voice rose. 'Where is he?'

Benedict drew an appreciative breath, for although heavy-featured, she was quite beautiful. She was Mexican with long legs, olive skin and enormous, wild eyes. She was bare-footed and a light blouse only just managed to contain the full breasts that were heaving with the force of her emotion. She looked as dangerous as a mountain cat as she glared at him from blazing eyes.

'Where is he? What have you done to Salazar?'

'I killed him.'

She leapt at him with a shriek, nails raking at his face. He side-stepped, housed his guns and seized her wrists as she twisted and came after him. She writhed violently and slammed a knee at his groin. He hipped aside, then bore down hard on her wrists.

'Relax, little one, relax.'

'You killed my man!' she screamed. 'I keel you.'

'Your man?' he challenged, conscious of the heavy scent of hot-bodied young woman rising up from her as she writhed against him. 'That's not so, little one. He wasn't a man – he was just a murderous dog.'

The girl got a hand free and slashed at his cheek. He grappled with her again and they wrestled about the clearing in tense and hard-breathing silence,

114

watched by the curious horse.

Then it didn't seem to be combat any more, but some sort of violent, sinuous dance. The wild girl got a hand free again but didn't scratch. The hand seized Benedict's hair at the back, pulling and twisting at it but somehow seeming to draw his head slowly towards her.

Benedict's taunting smile gave way to a different, burning look as he stared down into her liquid eyes, at the small, white clenched teeth. He bent her backwards. She didn't resist. He drew her hard against him. Her lips looked swollen and her throat was corded. He could feel the hardness of her nipples right through his coat.

'*Hombre!*' she cried suddenly, and they sank down together on the cushioning grass.

Dawn came to New Mexico with the night sky dying and coyotes calling from the purple hills. Smoke and river mist lay over the squalid Spanish town set at the base of a rearing bluff. From the southern end of the town a rusty water cart rumbled on its way to the river, stirring up the day's first dust.

On a balcony, a woman stood facing the rising sun, combing her hair with a big wooden comb and on her face was a look of seeing nothing. The ritual of a new day was under way.

From out of the trees came the two riders, the dew wet grass moving heavily under the hoofs. They drew rein and the girl extended a hand.

'Candelaria.'

Benedict nodded silently. It was a town like so many other Spanish towns along the border, though looking more squalid and decayed than the general run.

Like just about every Mexican town in that part of the country, Candelaria was built around a large plaza. The plaza was dominated by a small church with a ridiculously tall spire, and even it looked as if it were rotting into the ash-colored dust. He smiled wryly when the girl spoke again.

'Candelaria . . . that means candle of the road. It is pretty is it not?'

A pretty name for one hell of an ugly looking place, Benedict thought. But being a gentleman all he said was, 'Quite.' Then, 'Does Salazar have kinfolk here?'

'No, like me, he was alone.'

'Friends?'

The girl gave him a guarded look. 'Si.'

Benedict nodded, took out his cigar case and lit the day's first Havana and studied the girl.

Her name was Chata Escobar and she lived in Candelaria. It was when she'd revealed this, that he'd decided to accompany her home, as he'd intended visiting the town that day in any case. Chata had had no objections, the contrary in fact. She said she had a little cottage all her own and he was welcome to stay there for just as long as he liked.

Benedict had no delusions about hot-blooded

Chata, nor did he mistrust her. If there was one subject on which the gambling man considered himself an expert, it was women. He felt he understood Chata. The girl was an orphan in a hard case town. He had killed Salazar, he'd made love to her, now he was her protector. It was jungle law, but this was a primitive country.

'What are you thinking?' the girl said, catching his gaze.

Benedict ashed his cigar with a flick of the thumb. 'Why, I was thinking that you might tell me why Salazar tried to kill me.'

'That I do not know. I did not even know what he was doing.'

'You rode to Antigua with him and didn't know why?'

'Salazar seldom told me anything of his work. I do know that at many times he has killed many men.'

'Then can you tell me anything about the cattle rustling on the Rancho Antigua?'

The girl shook her raven tresses. 'No, I know nothing.'

'You're not convincing, Chata. I know Salazar was connected with the rustling, and you've been living with him. You must know all about it too.'

The girl moved her horse closer to his and looked up into his face intently.

'Hombre, I can say nothing to you. I take a great risk in even being seen with you.'

'Salazar can't hurt you now.'

'There are others as dangerous as Salazar.'

Benedict wanted to hear more about that but the girl held up her hands. 'No, that is all I am prepared to say. Even to talk sometimes is dangerous in Candelaria.'

Benedict let it go at that and they headed for the town. He was growing more sure as time went by, that Chata knew a great deal. He was confident he could get it out of her, but not if he rushed it. He could afford to be patient for a little time at least.

The sinister atmosphere of the town was even more noticeable as they rode across the square. Huddled adobe huts spread away on both sides, squat adobe ovens like a colony of huge beehives. Evil-eyed men watched their passing, slatternly women shrieked at naked children from open windows. They rode around the weed-choked, vacant lot flanking the old church and stopped before a small adobe house with green shutters and a sagging fence.

'My home,' said the girl. 'All I have in this world.' She led the way, barefoot, up the path and unlocked the door with a key taken from the pocket of her dress.

The house only boasted two rooms, kitchen and bedroom. It was cramped and gloomy but Benedict was pleased to note, rather cleaner than he might have expected.

The girl hustled about fixing breakfast, seemingly not one whit sorrowful about her recently departed paramour. Benedict smiled to himself as he shucked off his coat and stood at a window looking up towards the square. No, death would mean little here in Candelaria he figured. Either the death of a man like Salazar . . . or a gringo like him. . . .

Weariness overcame him as they ate tortillas and fat back. Yesterday had been a big day, last night long and dangerous. He would need to be fresh before seeing what he could dig up in sunny Candelaria.

'Is there a hotel in town, Chata? I need some sleep.'

'You would be much safer sleeping here, *hombre*,' she smiled, getting up from her chair and sliding her bare arms about his neck. 'This house is quite safe. The windows have catches and the door can be barred from within.'

He bent and kissed her. 'All right, I'll take your word for it. Coming?'

She returned his kiss with hot vigor but then drew back. 'No, first there are things I must attend to.'

'What sort of things?'

She spread her hands. 'As I told you, Salazar has friends here. If I did not go and at least tell them what happened, they would be suspicious and begin trouble. Already they would be suspicious on seeing you ride in with me.'

Benedict thought about that for a while, then nodded. 'Yes, I guess that makes sense. All right, but don't be too long. I mightn't be able to keep awake.'

'I will wake you, hombre – be sure of that.'

The girl left the house and made her way down to the plaza. She walked swiftly with a light, swinging stride, and was humming to herself. Far from mourning Salazar, she was relieved to be free of the man who had held her only through fear. By comparison with Salazar, the butcher, Benedict the gringo was almost a godlike man, the like of which she had never hoped to bring to her bed.

She stopped humming and put on a suitably somber expression when she approached the gallery of the store where Salazar's friends were sitting, silently smoking cornhusk cigarettes. Jaramillo, Ramirez and Lino Estevan watched her with bleak and hostile eyes as she came up the steps. She spoke directly to Estevan, a stocky, vicious-faced man of fifty who was perhaps the closest Salazar had had to a friend.

'Lino, I have bad news. Last night when . . .'

'We know what happened last night,' Estevan cut in, getting to his feet.

The girl's eyes widened. 'You know? But how?'

'A rider came in from the Antigua before you rode in with the gringo.'

Estevan's deep-set eyes glittered with bright malevolence. 'We know that the gringo Benedict murdered our *companero*, and that now he is at your house. You rode out with Salazar, you ride back with his killer. It would seem you do not mourn long, little Chata. It would seem perhaps that you are glad Salazar is dead.'

'No. It was not like that, Lino. You must understand that . . .'

Estevan smashed her across the face with the back of his hand with such force that she fell to the ground. Ramirez seized her by the shoulders and lifted her up. With blood trickling from the mouth, the girl's face showed a brief, primitive fury, then went white as she felt the cold, deadly prick of Jaramillo's knife against her soft throat.

She rolled her eyes, but dared not move. '*Por favor*,' she begged. 'I have done nothing.'

'Not as yet perhaps,' Estevan murmured coldly. 'But you will. You will help us kill the gringo pig, won't you, little Chata?'

'No, I . . .'

Now Estevan also had a knife in his hand and looked ready to use it. 'The gringo is to be killed. You will help us or we will cut your heart out. Maybe we will cut your heart out anyhow.'

Chata had turned a sour cream yellow with dark, half-moon shadows beneath her sick eyes. She was trembling like a leaf. She'd always known these three to be vicious scum, but they had never dared menace her because of Salazar. Now Salazar was gone and she was naked. Naked and terribly afraid.

'You will help us,' Estevan repeated.

The girl could hardly breathe, was incapable of thinking beyond the one thought. She didn't want to die.

'*Sí*,' she whispered at long length, her heart

feeling like a cold lump of stone. '*Sí* . . . I will do as you say.'

Perhaps it was a bad time to be thinking about vanishing beeves and not concentrating on what he was doing, Hank Brazos realized, as the horse he was breaking pelted him clear over the corral fence he was remembering his old man telling him that it never paid a man ever to think too much. That was how a man got himself into trouble, he used to warn him, and old Joe Brazos had never been guilty of thinking too much in his life.

Yet as Brazos hit the ground like a bale of cotton, bounced, and rolled to a dusty stop against the legs of an alarmed Pancho Pino, he realized that either the thinking or the spill had borne fruit. Suddenly there was the answer to what had been plaguing him right along.

'The other side of the river!' he breathed as the little fat Mexican assisted him to his feet and slapped huge clouds of dust off his clothes. He tweaked the Mexican's ear. 'That's it, you misbegotten son-of-a-Mexican-whore. It's got to be the other side of the river . . . that's the only place I haven't checked out.'

Pancho Pino looked very worried. 'Perhaps you should come seet down in the shade, Señor. That was a bad fall. Your head, by jeengs, I theenk you hit it too hard on the ground.'

Brazos shook the man's hands away impatiently, snapped his fingers at Bullpup, and headed for the stables. He reappeared in no time at all astride the appaloosa, headed for the main gate.

'Señor, where do you go?' Pino called after him. 'What of the work?'

Brazos made no response and kicked the horse into a lope. His round, fat face creased with worry and perplexity, Pino watched him out of sight, then shook his head, wonderingly. This Brazos must be a crazy man he thought.

So it was that some thirty minutes later, when Juan Romero rode in from the southern pastures where he'd been branding calves, he found no work going on at the corrals, and Pancho Pino sitting in the shade, whittling.

'What is going on here?' he demanded, swinging down. 'Where is Brazos?'

Pino jumped up and held the ramrod's horse. 'Señor Brazos went off on his horse, Juan.'

'Where did he go?'

'I know not . . . but he was saying something strange . . . something about the other side of the river.'

Romero paled. 'The other side of the river? Which direction did he take?'

Pino pointed. 'He was riding towards the Basin I teenk. Ees . . . ees something wrong, Juan?'

Juan Romero didn't answer, and Pino saw that his hands were trembling slightly as he turned away and led his horse across the yard. Reaching the gate, the ramrod stood there for several minutes looking southeast in the direction of the Bucksaws, torn with doubt, indecision and a mounting alarm.

Preoccupied, he didn't see the rider signaling down to him with his sombrero from the rise a half mile west of the headquarters. Finally the man was obliged to take out his six-gun and fire a shot at the sky. Romero mounted up and rode across the graze to the hill, where he spent some ten minutes listening to the ugly little Mexican who'd ridden over with the news that Duke Benedict had shown up in Candelaria with Chata Escobar.

Romero had been alarmed before, but alarm had been supplanted by a sharp sense of danger, and a realization that perhaps everything was in danger of exploding in his face.

'They know what to do with the gringo of course?' he demanded.

'*Sí*, Juan. Do not worry. Benedict will not leave Candelaria alive.'

That was some comfort to Romero as he dismissed the Mexican and rode slowly back towards the headquarters under a brilliant sun, but not much. It was evil luck, the man brooded bitterly, that Duke Benedict should have come to Antigua. He hadn't anticipated that. Larsen had been nothing; he'd been easy to get rid of. Benedict was dangerous, a different breed. The messenger from Candelaria had told him the others were preparing to take care of Benedict at Chata Escobar's house. If only he could be confident they could do it.

They had the numbers. They should succeed.

But if they failed?

The ramrod's eyes swung up to the great house which had been built by his grandfather fifty years ago. As always, the sight inspired him and he knew that no matter what happened, he could not weaken in his resolve to take Rancho Antigua, as many years before, Nathan Kendrick had taken it from his family.

Things were going bad and he could only hope that they wouldn't get worse, but if they did, then he would be forced to forget his scheme to drain and weaken Rancho Antigua and ultimately force Kendrick to sell out. Then it would have to become open war and should it come, he comforted himself with the knowledge of the two surprise weapons that could well carry him to victory.

Bo Rangle was one. Kendrick's own daughter was the other.

NINE

A HARD MAN
TO KILL

Benedict unlocked the door at Chata's knock. She started when she saw the gun in his hand, then smiled, tightly it seemed to Benedict.

'I expect a kiss, and you welcome me with a gun? Is this how it is to be with us, hombre?'

Benedict's white smile flashed in the gloom as he thrust the Peacemaker into the waistband of his trousers and rested his hands on her shoulders.

'I'll take kisses to Colts any old day,' he assured her, then proved it.

The girl, seemingly tense when she'd come in, quickly turned amorous. 'Everything is all right in the town,' she assured him, leading him by the hand into the bedroom. 'Nobody seems to care that

Salazar is dead, which is not surprising.' Reaching
the bedside, she slipped her hands around his slim
waist and pressed herself against him. Then she suddenly stepped back, frowning down at the gun in his
waistband. 'Please, put that away, hombre. Chata
hates guns.'

Benedict smiled and slipped the Colt into the
gunrig hanging around the bedpost. Then he took
her in his arms again and murmured, 'You were a
long time, Chata, I've been waiting . . .' And drew her
down onto the bed.

'*Muy hombre . . .*'

A furtive sound penetrated the fog of sleep. Benedict
sat up in bed. Chata was no longer lying beside him.
The sound came again.

It was a window being opened!

He left the bed as if fired from a catapult and burst
into the kitchen like a scalded wild cat.

Chata was thrusting the window up with one hand,
pushing his gunrig out with the other. He flung
himself across the room in one gigantic leap and
seized the gunbelt the split-second before it would
have fallen onto the verandah.

Hell erupted.

Chata screamed, a gun went off, the window burst
under the impact of a bullet, and running feet
sounded outside.

Benedict had both guns in his hands when a
stocky, shouting Mexican appeared at the window,

spraying shots into the room. Benedict drove three bullets through his wide open mouth, smashing him off the verandah, across the yard, and into the fence that crashed about him as he fell.

Benedict threw the open-mouthed girl one withering look, then flung himself low as a rear window was smashed open, and to the accompaniment of shouts and curses, somebody applied a shoulder to the flimsy rear door.

Benedict snapped a shot at the window and was rewarded with a yelp of pain. Then he concentrated on the shuddering door, and standing in a wide-legged crouch with lips skinned back from his teeth, emptied both guns through the woodwork, the sheer intensity of the fire blasting out a hat-sized piece of lumber and giving him a glimpse of a man with a crimson smear for a face turning slowly on his heels in a grotesque arabesque of death.

An arm, shoulder and rusty six-gun came through the shattered window and Benedict leapt for the cover of the bedroom doorway as thundering lead came hunting. Fingering fresh shells into his six-guns, he took quick stock of his situation then darted to the bedroom window. Working the clasp, he thrust it silently open and leaned out. There was only one man in sight, and he was standing at the next window yelling and shooting. He saw Benedict and spun. Benedict's gun coughed and the Mex went reeling back with a bullet in his shoulder. Deliberately Benedict shot him through the elbow, then the knee.

The man fell in a screaming heap in the grass and kicked at the earth.

On silent feet Benedict went through to the front and peered out. The yard and the street were empty save for the man with half a head lying in the wreckage of the fence. White faces showed at windows across the street, but nothing else. He went through to the back again, looked out at the dead man by the door, then at the crippled man in the grass. There had only been three of them.

Suddenly he whirled at a sound. Chata, who'd flung herself down when the fierce clash of arms erupted, was now crouched on the floor facing him, her face a white mask of shock and fear.

She was holding the rusty old gun that the bullet-crippled Mexican had dropped through the window. It was pointing at him.

'Drop it, Chata.'

Agonizing indecision twisted the girl's face. The grisly conflict of the past minute had driven home to her with bloody impact, that she was a Mexican girl in a Mexican town and this handsome gringo was the enemy, as all gringos were. If she did not shoot, the gringo would soon be gone and she would just be little Chata – the girl who had betrayed her own. She wanted to shoot, but it was so hard . . . so hard when his arms had held her in a way she had never been held before . . .

'Drop the gun or I will kill you, Chata.'

He meant it.

A sob broke from her throat as the rusty old gun thudded to the floor. Benedict crossed the room and picked it up. He stared down at her bowed head, eyes chill and remote. She lifted her eyes, winced when she saw the way he looked at her.

'Please, Señor, I am sorry. They made me do it.'

Benedict thrust the gun into his belt and turned away. He went through to the bedroom, donned coat, boots and hat, then kicked his way through what was left of the back door and went out to the man lying in the grass.

He was as ugly as mortal sin and glared up at the tall American with eyes blurred by tears, pain and hatred.

'What's your name, scum?'

The man spat at him. Benedict kicked him in the face, then stamped on his bullet-shattered arm.

When the man finished screaming he said, 'Your name?'

'Lino Estevan. In the name of the Mother of God . . . mercy . . .'

Benedict hunkered down beside him, keeping his two guns in his hands, not because of Lino Estevan, but in case he had more friends.

'You know everything, don't you, Estevan,' he said softly. 'You know all about Salazar and the rustling on Rancho Antigua and Boyd Larsen and Bo Rangle . . . everything, don't you? And you're going to tell me all about it.'

Half swooning with pain, the Mexican nodded. '*Sí*

. . . *sí* . . . I know.'

A flicker of triumph touched Benedict's eyes. 'All right, my ugly friend, talk.'

Lino Estevan talked and Duke Benedict listened in growing amazement. Yet he never doubted the man for a moment, for everything he said tied in with everything he had so far learned and guessed about Rancho Antigua.

'All right, Estevan, we are riding back to the Antigua and there you will tell Nathan Kendrick everything you have told me, *compre?*'

With scant regard for the man's condition, Benedict loaded him onto a horse that one of his companions had ridden down from the square and tethered in the alley behind the house. Then he saddled up the black and mounted, taking up the lines of the sagging Mexican's mount.

He looked towards the house.

Chata stood in the bullet-riddled doorway. She no longer looked lusty and desirable, but somehow small and beaten and lost. She lifted a hesitant hand in farewell, but the tall man in black made no response.

Benedict touched his spurs to the black and rode out. He made his way down the staring street with a hundred eyes watching and not one man dared lift a finger against him. He turned out of the street where men had died and crossed the square, passing through the shadows of the tall Spanish church.

He rode out of Candelaria and took the trail for

131

Rancho Antigua. And only when the little town was far behind did he turn in his saddle, and touching fingers to hat brim, murmured softly,

'*Adios*, Chata.'

Hank Brazos stood in the blazing sun under the towering cliffs on the narrow rocky bank on the southern side of Slave River whistling through his teeth.

Bullpup didn't appear.

The big man swore to himself and started clambering over the rocks in the direction the dog had gone. Since swimming the appaloosa across to the cliff side of the river, Brazos had spent some twenty minutes fruitlessly searching for something, anything, that could have offered an exit for stolen cattle from Sweetwater Basin. So far all he'd found were rocks and more rocks, and now he seemed to have lost an ugly dog.

'Bullpup!' he shouted, and the echoes bounced off the beetling cliffs above. 'Here!'

He waited. The dog didn't appear.

Growing a little concerned now, Brazos pushed on another fifty yards until suddenly the familiar ringing trail cry of the dog sounded muffled from somewhere ahead. Brazos grinned and quickened his pace. By the sound of it, Bullpup had found something.

Moments later the dog ran into sight from behind a towering shelf of rock some fifty yards long that was split off from the cliff face as if by a giant knife. Between the shelf and the cliff, was a passage some ten feet wide. Thick in the air here was the unmistakable smell of cattle. The earth was torn by many hoofs, and squarely behind the shelf, totally concealed from sight from the far bank, was a deep cleft in the wall of the cliffs.

'Why you flea-bitten, kitchen-robbin' old pot licker,' Brazos breathed as he stared into the dark crevice. 'You danged well found it!'

Bullpup wagged his stumpy tail proudly and they walked into the gloomy corridor of stone. They followed it some fifty yards until it opened into a high-walled canyon. The tracks of hundreds of cattle, old and new, stretched away before them along the canyon floor.

'Remind me to find you a marrow bone when we get back to headquarters, ugly,' Brazos grinned, spun, and trotted back towards the river to get his horse.

Making his way back along the narrow bank, Brazos could see how easy the whole thing could be for the rustlers. The stolen cattle would be swum across the Slave, driven up behind the shelf, through the cleft and into the canyon leaving behind nothing to warrant any rustler-hunting vaquero sparing this stretch of cliff face so much as a passing glance.

It took some time to get the appaloosa along the rocks, but once he got back to the cleft where Bullpup waited, he was able to mount up and ride through to the canyon.

Brazos whistled between his teeth in appreciation of the size and beauty of the secret canyon. The walls on either side were up to a thousand feet high, the canyon so narrow, that there would be parts where the sun never reached the bottom except at noon. Much of the canyon bottom was choked with a thick growth of brush on either side of the clear cattle track that stretched before him. There were clear, cold pools of water, supplied by small streams trickling down from a number of springs higher up the canyon. As he rode on the canyon widened and he saw deeper pools, shaded by little cottonwoods, aspen and an occasional fir.

Where the sunlight touched the higher walls of the canyon, it turned the sandstone and limestone walls to beautiful colors, stained by water and streaked by salt.

He followed the canyon for some three miles, winding deep into the heart of the Bucksaws. He halted only when he sighted a sentry's silhouetted frame against the sky a long way ahead. The man hadn't seen him yet, but by his vigilant posture, Brazos knew that he was alert and that there was no way of getting near him without being sighted.

Hunkering down by a great boulder that bulked amongst a group of willows trailing over a still, cold pond, he built a cigarette and considered whether he should risk going on or heading back and making contact with Benedict. It was finally the approaching darkness that prompted him to take the latter course. He mounted up, retraced his path to the cavern, swam the Slave again, then pointed the appaloosa's head for the homestead. Darkness engulfed him before he got clear of the basin and he figured it would be a couple of hours before the moon came up. He rode easy in the saddle, his mind busy with his momentous discovery. At last he knew how they'd been getting the cattle away; doubtless that secret canyon finally led into the badlands somewhere. But what he still didn't know was who was behind it.

Stars were beginning to show, point by point, in the night sky when he heard the sound of many hoofs far off to the north. He stopped and stood in the stirrups but could see nothing. The horsemen pounded by in the blackness about a mile distant by the sound of it, then dropped suddenly out of earshot as they dipped down into Sweetwater Basin.

Shrugging, he built a new cigarette and gigged the horse into a gallop and held him to it all the way back to the ranch house to find the place ablaze with lights and in a storm of confusion.

'What the hell?' he breathed as he spun through the gate and across the main yard, almost running down a vaquero sprinting for the stables. He yelled at the man but he didn't stop. He kept on, swinging down in front of the house just as the little Pancho Pino came running out. The little man gasped in fright when the iron hand seized him, then went limp with relief when he saw who it was.

'Oh, Señor Brazos I thought . . .'

'What the hell's goin' on?' he demanded.

Pancho Pino made the Sign of the Cross on his chest. 'Madre de Dios, Señor Brazos, bad theengs. Romero, he shoot the patron and flee with many of the men.'

'Kendrick shot?'

'*Sí, sí.*' Pino gestured down the hallway. 'He ees in the house with Señorita Brenda and . . . the insurance man.'

'The Yank's here?' said Brazos, then not waiting for an answer, ran down the hall and burst into the front room.

Nathan Kendrick lay on a leather sofa, ashen-faced and naked to the waist. Duke Benedict was bent over him, bandaging up a bloody wound in his chest. White-faced servants were running around in confusion with bandages and hot water. Behind the sofa, Brenda stood with her hands pressed to her face, sobbing quietly.

Relief showed in Benedict's face when he looked up.

'Nice timing, Reb.' Then, in response to Brazos' quizzical glance at the others. 'It's all right. I've told them we're working together now . . .'

'Just a minute,' Brazos cut in. 'What's goin' on here, Yank?'

'Not just now, Reb. First I want you to hustle out and see to it that all hands are fully armed and ready to ride. You attend to that while I finish patching Nathan up, then I'll explain things.'

Brazos grunted and disappeared. It took him some time to calm the excited vaqueros down and get them saddled, but a squad of thirty heavily-armed men were drawn up outside by the time he returned to the house where Benedict was just putting the finishing touches to Kendrick's bandages.

'All set, Reb?'

'All set.' Brazos' face creased with perplexity. 'Yank, Pino tells me Romero plugged Mr. Kendrick. Is that so?'

'It's so right enough, Brazos,' the cattle king panted. 'The dirty Judas Mex polecat tried to do me in – after bleedin' me all these months.' He shot a bitter eye at his sobbing daughter. 'Stole my cattle, my daughter, and then tried to take my life . . . goddam his greaser eyes.'

'Please, father, don't,' the girl sobbed.

Brazos looked in puzzlement from one to the other, and only then noticed the ugly Mexican stretched on bloody blankets in an adjoining room.

'Who the hell's that?'

'His name's Lino Estevan,' Benedict explained. 'He and a few more like him tried to kill me in Candelaria. They didn't have any luck, and with just a little persuasion, Señor Estevan revealed that he and his companions were associates of our friend Salazar, and up to their greasy scalps in the rustling.'

Brazos was all ears. 'Go on.'

'A fantastic story, Reb. Romero, it seems, believes he has some right to the Rancho Antigua because Kendrick supposedly took it off his grandfather by force back in the days when land titles didn't mean anything. According to Estevan, Romero came here, got a job and worked his way up to ramrod specifically to place himself in a position where he would one day be able to take over the ranch.'

'Well I'll be dogged.'

'Yes indeed. Apparently Romero's plan was to marry Brenda and ultimately come by the Antigua that way.'

'You mean Romero and Miss Brenda are . . .'

Benedict nodded soberly, his eyes on the still crying girl. 'Romantically involved, shall we say. But apparently Romero had to change his plans when he discovered that Kendrick would never permit his daughter to marry a Mex. That happened a few months ago, I believe, when Romero had Brenda discreetly sound the old man out on the possibility of her getting married.'

'Yeah, Kendrick ain't exactly got a high opinion of Mexes, I've noticed.'

'That's right. Well, when Romero realized this, he conceived the idea of rustling the Antigua. He planned to bleed it white and drive Kendrick to ruin and then buy him out for next to nothing. That was where Salazar came in. Romero made contact with Salazar and Estevan and a few others and put the proposition to them. Romero said he would tell them

138

when and where to strike, how to get rid of the beeves and he could guarantee that they wouldn't run into any danger.'

'And Salazar jumped at the bait?'

'Not right off. You see, traditionally, rustling from the Rancho Antigua has always been a fatal sort of a business. No, it wasn't until Romero told Salazar about some secret canyon, only he knew about, leading out of Sweetwater Basin that would make the rustling easy, that . . .'

'I know the place on account I just come back from there.'

Benedict's eyes widened. 'You found it? Damn, but that's great, Reb, on account Estevan's too far gone to sit a saddle now and we could have wasted all night looking for it. Damn good work.'

Brazos tapped his temple modestly with his finger, then said, 'Keep goin', Yank, I'm followin' most of it. So Salazar took on the job after he found out about the canyon?'

'Yes he did. They ran off a small herd to start with, drove it off through the badlands and sold it down at Mescalero. But things didn't really get under way in earnest until Bo Rangle showed up.'

'Then he is in it?'

'Up to his neck. You see, Rangle was kicked out of Texas by the law and he found his way here. He teamed up with Salazar and set about rustling Antigua stock in earnest, setting up headquarters in Romero's secret canyon. They sold the beeves through a Mexican dealer named Lobato in Mescalero, though Estevan tells me that a certain Arrillaga pushed Lobato out and took over that end of the arrangements. Estevan has since heard a rumor that Arrillaga was killed by Rangle and Lobato is handling the cattle again.'

'That sounds like Rangle.'

'Indeed it does. And the deal suited both Rangle and Romero. Rangle had the beeves and he could keep whatever they brought, and at the same time, raids were weakening the Antigua. All Romero was interested in was breaking Kendrick so he could take over.'

'Some story, Yank. And you say Rangle's in that canyon?'

'That's right, and we're goin' to flush him out tonight. But to get on with the story, it seems everything went well until Larsen showed up and started sniffing about. Larsen bribed one of Estevan's friends, Keechez, who told him about Rangle. That's why they killed Larsen in Sabinosa that night, and they didn't waste any time cutting Keechez's throat and tossing him in the river. Then it was back to business as usual again until you and I appeared on the scene.'

'Yeah, I reckon things are beginnin' to add up now. Now I know why Romero was so proddy.'

'That's right. He sat back and watched as long as he could, but when it began to look tight, he hired Salazar to kill me. When I killed Salazar, Romero sent a man to Candelaria to tell Estevan and the others that I planned to visit over there. They were still digesting the news when I arrived with Salazar's girl-friend. Well, as I told you, they tried to kill me then, but it didn't pan out that way.'

He exhaled blue cigar smoke at the ceiling, and went on.

'I brought Estevan here to repeat the story he told me at Candelaria. Romero must have seen us coming, for he suddenly disappeared. Estevan had just told Kendrick what he'd told to me, when Romero came up from the bunkhouses with about ten of the vaqueros who've been in with him on the whole deal. Before we could stop him, Kendrick went charging out in a rage with a gun and Romero shot him. I gunned down two of Romero's boys and when some of Kendrick's loyal cowboys came in on my side, Romero saw the game was up and they high-tailed it. It's my guess they've headed for the canyon.'

'That's no guess. A passel of riders passed me headin' for the basin as I was comin' in. Must have been Romero.'

'That caps it then. All right, let's get going. I hope you're in fighting mood, Reb, on account, from my estimate, Romero and Rangle together would be able to saddle about thirty men. We'd have about that many here, but they're vaqueros, not gunmen.'

'Give me a smell of Bo Rangle and I'm a fightin' fool any day of the week,' Brazos assured him. He looked at Nathan Kendrick, then turned accusing eyes on the girl.

'I didn't know about the rustling,' she protested. 'I didn't know what Juan was doing . . . but I still love him.'

Her words brought a curse to Nathan Kendrick's lips and then he shuddered and went limp.

Kneeling at the man's side to feel his pulse, Benedict said, 'He'll pull through, but don't leave his side until the medic gets here, Brenda.'

'I'm not staying, I'm going with you,' the girl said rebelliously, rushing to the door. 'I still don't believe all those terrible things you said about Juan. I'll want to see him and to stop you from killing him if I can. The women will take care of father.'

Benedict shrugged as the girl ran out. 'I suppose she has the right to come in a way. All right, Reb, let's raise dust.'

They left the house at a run and leapt astride their horses that the vaqueros were holding waiting for them. A brief glance at the long, heavily-armed and sober-faced squad of riders waiting for them, and then they were leading the way through the gate and thundering swiftly towards the rising moon.

TEN

BATTLE OF GHOST CANYON

It was strangely cold in the place they called Ghost Canyon, and even the newly risen moon that climbed over the towering battlements of stone above the outlaws' camp and drenched the rocky shelves before the caverns with metallic light, seemed chill and unfriendly.

Below the stone shelves on which the men were gathered in dark and silent knots watching Bo Rangle, a little stream chattered and gurgled in the black caverns of moon shadow. Down there, porous rocks were never touched by the sun and slimy water seeped down to spread through dark moss. Sometimes Ghost Canyon could be a pretty place by day, but never by night.

There were some thirty men on the ledges, a long string of saddled horses. Saddles and camping gear were strewn about and a large fire burned where Rangle's riders had been roasting a hindquarter of beef when the Rancho Antigua men had come in a minute before. Never particularly friendly despite a common cause, the two ranks were even more markedly divided than ever now, with the Antigua men standing on one rock step up behind Juan Romero and the hard-bitten hellers of Rangle's Raiders dotted across a lower ledge beyond their angry leader.

Rangle's men were mostly Americans, lean and dangerous-looking hellions with crossed ammunition belts strung across their chests and tied-down guns. The killer breed.

Every man started just a little as Bo Rangle suddenly punched his palm with a sound like a muffled rifle shot.

'Benedict and Brazos!' His voice shook with venom. He made the names sound like an epithet. 'Damn their eyes – aren't I ever goin' to be rid of that pair of scum?'

'You know them?' Juan Romero showed his astonishment.

Hatless in the moonlight, Bo Rangle turned a brutal, bitter face at the ramrod.

'Know them? Of course I know them. They've been doggin' my trail ever since the War. That's what they're doin' down here goddammit, lookin' for me.'

Romero digested that startling piece of information as he watched the killer prowl to and fro like a caged cat. Then he brightened.

'By the Virgin, this is even better, Rangle. Now you have as much reason as I, to ride against the Antigua.'

Rangle stopped his tigerish pacing and halted before the wide-shouldered Mexican.

'Join you against Antigua?' he said, puzzled. 'What are you talkin' about?' So far Romero had only told him of developments back at the ranch headquarters earlier that evening, not of the ramrod's plans that he'd conceived during the ride out to the secret canyon.

'Why, we must now ride together and destroy Kendrick and all his power,' Romero said logically. 'Now, tonight, is the time to do it. With our combined forces it shall be easy, for the best fighters on the ranch are the loyal men here with me. Kendrick is wounded and . . .'

'You're loco, Mex.'

Romero blinked. 'I do not understand, Rangle.'

Bo Rangle laughed, a tearing sound that bounced up off the lofty ramparts.

'Then I'll spell it out to you, ramrod. All I'm interested in is beeves, not settin' you up on your goddam throne. I told you that from the jump. Well now, thanks to your bunglin', the rustlin's got to fold – and just when I had it all set up right in Mescalero too. You want to wipe Kendrick out, you wipe him

145

out. Me? I'm haulin' my freight with that herd down to Mescalero. After that I dunno. Maybe Mexico for a spell ... but one thing's for sure, companero, I won't be showin' back here. I'm still short of the funds I'm goin' to need to handle a big job I got in mind.'

'But I still don't understand. If you ride with me tonight I can give you a vast reward.' Romero paused, searching for the right inducement. 'Rangle, you come with me to crush Antigua and I shall give you half the entire ranch. Now is that not reason enough for you to join me?'

'It sure as hell ain't. I told you at the start, all I'm interested in is gettin' the stake. Well, I've got my stake and I'm not gettin' my boys shot to ribbons just so you can play ranchero, Mex. Besides, rustlin' beeves ain't takin' on a big ranch, mister. That caper just leads to the long rope.' He spun on his heel. 'C'mon, boys, let's get movin'.'

'No, do not leave,' Romero shouted. 'You must fight with us! I will pay five hundred dollars to every man who fights with me.'

Bo Rangle halted and his eyes were dangerous. 'You tryin' to buy my men off me, Mex. I said we're goin'.'

'But you must not go.' Juan Romero seemed in the grip of an emotion stronger than himself as he spread his hands and tried to make them understand. 'Rangle, the Antigua is mine by right of birth. It was stolen from my forefathers by American guns.

146

For years I have worked and slaved and been called greaser and lived under the gringo heel, only so that one day it would be mine again as it was my forefathers. Can you understand what it has been like for me? To know that I am only kept on at the ranch because I work harder than any two men there, to risk losing the woman I love to the first good-looking gringo who comes along, to . . .'

He broke off as Bo Rangle's harsh laugh sounded again.

'Boy, you got more wrinkles than a rattler, Romero. Now it's Benedict you're after. You can't make up your mind . . .'

'No!' Romero cut in fiercely. 'He's not important. Only the ranch is important.'

Rangle spoke quietly. 'Take a word of friendly advice, Romero. Saddle up and git gone just like we're aimin' to do. When a hand's played out, it's played out. OK, boys.'

The outlaws turned to go. Juan Romero stared after them with blazing eyes for an electric second, then suddenly swept out his gun.

'Rangle!'

Bo Rangle's face was glacial as he turned slowly to stare at the naked Colt. He lifted a restraining hand as his men made instinctive moves towards their six-guns.

'Just take it easy, boys, Señor Romero ain't goin' to plug anybody, are you, Romero?'

Romero curled back the hammer of his gun with

an ominous click. 'Only if you make me, Rangle. You shall stay.'

'Not a chance.' Bo Rangle shook his head. 'I'm goin', Mex, just like I said.'

'Then I shall kill you.'

'Maybe you will. Maybe you won't.' Rangle's deep voice was totally even; cowardice was not one of his many weaknesses. He started to back slowly towards his men. 'OK, boys, like Señor Romero says, he might kill me. If he does, then this is my last order. You're to shoot every mother's son, compre?'

A score of hard heads nodded, twenty violent hands rested on gun butts, twenty pairs of eyes drilled at Juan Romero . . .

Rangle backed away five paces. Another five. Behind Romero, the fighting cream of Rancho Antigua waited in sweaty tension, each man aware that the bullet that killed Bo Rangle could kill them all.

A shot rang down Ghost Canyon.

But Juan Romero's gun remained unfired, and he, along with every other man, swung his gaze north along the canyon where the shot had come from. In the echoing wake of the gunshot, they suddenly heard the rumble of many hoofs.

Juan Romero lowered his gun slowly, shaking his head. 'No, it couldn't be . . . they couldn't have found the entrance yet . . .'

'You want to believe that, you believe it, Mex,' Bo Rangle shouted, his gun in his fist now as he led his men for the horses. 'Us, we're makin' dust.'

Romero didn't even glance their way. His eyes were fixed along the canyon. Even the swift clatter of Rangle's riders as they swept away couldn't completely drown out the increasing rumble of hoofs heading towards them somewhere through the vast black caverns of moon shadow. It was the Antigua men. Another minute and they would be here . . .

For a moment Juan Romero's wide shoulders slumped and there was a taste like ashes in his mouth. But only for a moment, for suddenly he was realizing that he didn't really need Bo Rangle. Certainly the cavalcade of riders sweeping towards him through the night was thirty strong. But thirty what? Vaqueros, laborers, house servants. Certainly they had the numbers, but he had the quality . . .

His shoulders straightened and the light of hope kindled in his eyes again as he turned and looked at his men. They were the cream of Rancho Antigua, men whose pride matched his, who shared his dream of restoring Rancho Antigua to its rightful owners. Its rightful Mexican owners.

'Companeros,' he said quietly. 'It is the hour of decision for us. You have shared my dream, followed my leadership and believed in ultimate victory. You are warriors like I am a warrior and the time has come to fight, to run or to die. What is it to be?'

A long moment of silence with the drum roll of hoofs growing rapidly closer passed. Then Francisco Semora, Romero's hatchet-faced *Segundo*, stepped forward.

'I fight with you, *companero*.'

'And I.'

'And I, *companero*.'

Every man stepped forward, and Juan Romero exulted. He made a sweeping gesture. 'All right, companeros, let us fight then. For Rancho Antigua! We shall fight for it, we shall win it, and we shall hold it by the same manner that Nathan Kendrick has held it, with our strength and our purpose.'

The words set his men afire. Swiftly and purposefully they drove their horses back into the caves, grabbed up their rifles and took up positions. In each man now burned Romero's Mexican dream of triumph over the gringo, and over their rifle sights they watched the first of the Antigua horsemen sweep into range.

'Tonight we fight for our heritage, *companeros*!' Juan Romero cried from behind a tall, yellow finger of stone a little above them. 'Fire!'

Ten guns crashed as one, their voice like a thunderclap from the gods as it smashed and rolled down Ghost Canyon.

Riders fell to their left and right under that first snarling volley, but shoulder to shoulder, Benedict and Brazos thundered on. They flashed by dark rock patches and gleaming mescal, six-guns drawn but yet unfired. Behind them a horse screamed in bowel-torn agony and horse and rider went crashing over, spilling and breaking down a slope. A man cried out in a high falsetto and a glancing bullet made a sound like a screaming train whistle. The air was alive with whipping lead and death and men screamed without knowing they screamed, and men died without a sound.

A dozen men fell in that first, bloody half-minute, and from his high point Juan Romero watched and waited for them to falter.

They didn't falter. Alone they might have, but now with their guns fiercely answering back Romero's fire, Benedict and Brazos were there to lead, to inspire, to keep them coming on when every screaming nerve and death fear wanted them to reef their horses' heads about.

Had the attackers hesitated, all would have been lost, but behind the flaming guns of the two tall gringos, they kept on even as more men and horses went down. The gringos obviously were mad, but their madness was infectious ... and *companero* do you not notice there is something glorious in their madness also. . . ?

But Hank Brazos and Duke Benedict weren't mad. They merely believed that the end of their long and bloody hunt for Bo Rangle was at hand. That was the spur that drove them through that lethal rain of lead and death, right up the rocky slopes of the outlaw hideout itself.

Romero's men began to panic in the face of the relentless charge as the swarming riders swept in close. One jumped cover and ran. Duke Benedict's gun flared, the man leapt high into the air like a shot antelope, somersaulted, and vanished into the black pits of shadow far below. Francisco Semora and Jose Mariano made a break back for the caves, firing from the hip as they ran. Hank Brazos, huge and frightening in the moonlight, burst around a rocky cleft and shot Semora through the head. Mariano's gun coughed back spitefully and Brazos spun out of the saddle, smashed hard against the unyielding stone, then bounced and rolled behind the protection of a corpse. Ignoring a bloody shoulder, he blasted a running Mexican into eternity then ducked as vicious lead came hunting him from Juan Romero's gun.

Now the entire rocky slope before the cave was fogged with gunsmoke, the air thick with the screams of the wounded and dying. In a shattering minute, Juan Romero saw his lifetime's ambition crumble and fall, broken apart on the iron guns of the two gringos.

Suddenly Romero glimpsed Benedict spurring after one of his fleeing men and driving him into the ground with his gun barrel. Somehow in that moment, the dashing Benedict seemed to represent to the defeated man, all the American enemies of his life, the crystallization of all his hate. He had lost, but to take Benedict with him would be to salvage something . . .

Benedict didn't even see Romero leaping from cover. All he heard was a warning shout from Brazos, then felt the bullet smash into his horse. With a scream, the animal reeled sideways, lost its footing and plummeted over a fifteen-foot drop. Benedict hit the ground with stunning force, rolled, tried to get up but couldn't make it. Above, Romero was sprinting towards the edge of the drop with a hungry gun. Fifty yards away, Brazos was getting to his feet, knowing even then that it would be too late. Romero reached the edge, breathed some fervent curse in Spanish and swung his gun towards the stunned figure sprawled on the rocks below.

A rifle spoke from below and beyond where Duke Benedict lay. Juan Romero shook, gun tumbling from his fist to strike a rock and bounce and land at Benedict's feet. He hugged himself as though terribly cold, lifted his face to the moon, then spun slowly and fell, his body landing with a dead-meat thud across Benedict's horse.

By the time the panting Brazos had reached the top of the drop, Duke Benedict was back on his feet and Brenda Kendrick, a rifle in her hands, was climbing up towards the ledge, her face a white mask of grief and shock.

'Did I ... did I kill him, Duke?' she cried. 'Is he...?'

'Yes, Brenda,' Benedict said quietly. 'He's dead. You ... you saved my life.'

The rifle dropped with a clatter from the girl's hand. 'I couldn't let him kill you. He was wrong ... Juan was terribly wrong ... but I did love him so ...'

She went to the dead man then, and kneeling beside him, took his head in her lap. Benedict looked down at her with a haggard face for a long moment, then turned and made his way slowly up to where Brazos stood. The shot that had killed Juan Romero had been the last of the battle. Romero's men were all dead or fled and the gunsmoke was rising eerily against the moon. Men moaned in agony, others lay quiet waiting for death. Figures stumbled about with a look of glazed shock, and some knelt to help those who had fallen.

'Well, we won,' Brazos said quietly without a hint of triumph in his voice as he packed a bandanna inside his shirt against his shoulder to staunch the flow of blood.

'Yeah,' nodded Benedict, his tone matching the others as he looked slowly about them. 'We won . . .'

'Rangle ain't here. That must have been him we seen kickin' up the dust as we was comin' in. But he can't be far gone. We goin' after him?'

Brazos fully expected the answer to be yes, for when it came right down to cases, Duke Benedict was more fervently dedicated to the cause of running down Bo Rangle than himself. His face broke into a smile when Benedict, after a long, difficult moment of decision, shook his head.

'No, we'll have to let him go. These people need us here.'

Brazos rested a hand on his shoulder. 'You know, Yank, sometimes you just about convince me you've got a heart after all.'

Duke Benedict made no reply, and for a long time after Brazos had turned and shambled away to help with the wounded, he remained looking down at the bowed figure of Brenda Kendrick holding her dead lover in her arms.

It was hot in Henry Gordon's office despite the fact that the windows and door stood open to catch any small breeze. Wearing a high starched collar and a wondering expression, Gordon sat totally absorbed in the strange tale of Rancho Antigua.

Duke Benedict sat opposite the desk, in tailored suit, bed-of-flowers vest, highly polished tan boots and an aromatic Havana. Benedict's clean-shaven face glowed with perfect health, revealing nothing of the rigors of the two weeks since they had last sat in this office.

When Benedict was finished, Gordon shook his head and sipped at his coffee which had been brought in minutes before by Miss Hunter who'd almost spilled a pot of coffee in his lap while smiling at Benedict.

'An amazing story . . . truly an amazing story. One can almost feel a sympathy for Romero despite the fact that what he did was criminal and wrong.' He set his cup down. 'Well, Mr. Benedict, the least I can say is that you've conducted this whole matter in a way that can only reflect the highest credit upon Southwest Insurance and all the high ideals it stands for.' He reached into a drawer and drew out two manila envelopes. 'I contracted to pay you fifty dollars a week, Mr. Benedict. In view of what you have achieved however, here is two hundred dollars in cash apiece. By the way, where is Mr. Brazos now?'

'He's across the street talking to Miss Larsen,' Benedict replied, putting the money in the inside pocket of his coat. 'I appreciate your generosity, Mr. Gordon. This money will take us a long way on Bo Rangle's trail.'

'Still determined to hunt that renegade, Mr. Benedict?'

'Why, of course.'

Gordon got to his feet and slid his fingers into his waistcoat pockets.

'Mr Benedict, I have a proposition I'd like to put to you, but first do you mind if I'm a little frank with you?'

'Certainly not.'

'Well, that day you gentlemen first came to my office, I must admit I had grave misgivings about putting you on the Southwest's payroll.'

Benedict smiled easily as he rose and picked up his black hat.

'Quite understandable, Mr. Gordon.'

'But my misgivings have proved to be totally without foundation. You resolved this difficult and perplexing affair in a manner totally in keeping with the highest standards set by this company. The question I want to put to you, is would you be prepared to forsake your hunt for Rangle and consider working for Southwest Insurance on a permanent basis?'

'I'm sorry, Mr Gordon.'

Gordon's face fell.

'You won't accept my offer?'

'Not won't, Mr Gordon. Can't.'

Gordon managed to conceal his disappointment, but as they made their way through the office to the street, he was sharply aware that but for a man named Bo Rangle, Southwest might have acquired two men who had capabilities to become the best investigators Southwest had ever had.

Seated at the front window of the Silver Spoon Eatery, Brazos saw Benedict and Gordon emerge from the insurance company and heaved a sigh of regret.

'Well, Miss Helen, there's my pard. Looks like it's time to ride.'

Helen Larsen, a far different girl from the grieving young woman who'd sat across this very table from him two weeks ago, reached out and touched his big brown hand.

'I'm very grateful to you, Hank. For everything.'

'Shucks, I didn't do so much, Miss Helen. And like I say, it was Benedict who nailed your brother's killer.'

'And your telling me that only confirms my first opinion of you, Hank. You're a fine, good and honest young man.'

Brazos couldn't help but blush.

'Heck, Miss Helen, them's mighty nice words, but I don't see as how they fit somehow.'

'No, I really mean it.' She smiled. 'Do you have to leave so soon? I mean, you have been through a lot, and you've been wounded. Couldn't you stay on in Summit just a few days? I promise I would take good care of you.'

For a moment as he met her blue eyes, Hank Brazos wavered. But then he dragged his gaze away and looked across the street. Benedict was already mounted up, the appaloosa was stamping impatiently at the rack. The trail was waiting . . . the trail of Bo Rangle, and a king's ransom in gold . . .

'I'm sorry, Miss Helen, but I can't.'

Somehow she seemed to understand. They rose in silence and went out onto the porch. Brazos adjusted the black calico sling on his arm, perched his battered hat on the back of his head and looked down at her. Suddenly she rose on tiptoes and kissed him on the lips. He lifted his big rough hand and touched her cheek wonderingly, then abruptly swung away and tramped across the street.

Reaching his horse, he glanced back and was surprised to see Bullpup still standing on the porch beside the girl.

'Come on, drat you,' he said almost angrily. 'Don't you understand we got to go.'

Bullpup lifted his scarred and ugly head and stared up at the girl. She crouched down and patted his head. He licked her hand with a big pink tongue, then jumped down off the walk and followed the two riders pulling away from the hitch rack.

'Some towns seem harder to leave than others, Reb,' Benedict murmured, looking back at the girl.

'Some towns are plain painful to leave,' Brazos growled back, and heeled his horse into a trot.

Henry Gordon crossed the street to stand with the girl watching them go, and as the horsemen crossed the river bridge, the little businessman felt a sharp pang of regret. Somehow those two tall men had brought into his neat and ordered life, a smell of something bigger, of wild and open places and a life of high adventure that rich little insurance men only ever dreamed about . . .

A big freighter wagon loaded with buffalo hides passed behind the receding riders, throwing up a billow of thick yellow dust. Henry Gordon and Helen Larsen strained their eyes for a last glimpse as the dust slowly blew away, but Hank Brazos and Duke Benedict were gone in the heat and the haze of the Apache Plains.